AF394804

Bedraggling Grandma with Russian Snow

João Reis

Title: Bedraggling Grandma with Russian Snow
Original title: *A Avó e a Neve Russa*
Copyright © João Reis, 2021

Published by Corona/Samizdat, Izola, Slovenia

Book design by © Célia Loureiro

Proofread by Justine Kaufmann
Funded by the DGLAB/Culture and the Ca-
mões, IP – Portugal

CIP - Kataložni zapis o publikaciji
Narodna in univerzitetna knjižnica, Ljubljana

821.134.3-31

REIS, João
Bedraggling Grandma with Russian Snow / João
Reis. – Izola : Corona Samizdat, June 2021

ISBN: 978-961-95196-8-4
COBISS.SI-ID: 66958083

Bedraggling Grandma with Russian Snow

João Reis

CORONA\SAMIZDAT

Dad was supposed to be dead or alive in an unknown location. On several occasions he told us he was in an unknown location, Bruce told the two detectives. If someone asks you, I'm in an unknown location, Dad would tell Alexei, but at 10.12 a.m. that day, it was last Saturday, yes, on Saturday Dad finished eating his waffle, dear gentlemen, and still at 10.12 a.m., but a few seconds later, he raised a hand to call the waitress, "One more waffle for the kid", he said. The kid was our Alexei, Bruce explained to the two detectives. The waitress looked at Dad, picked up his empty plate and went over to the counter to shout out "one more waffle". A big man stuck his head out of the small window in the wall and disappeared back inside it. Dad banged his open hand on the table, stuck his tongue through his teeth, sucked one cheek and whistled. We prefer Monsieur Béranger's establishment, our Alexei and I, but our father prefers that cafeteria with the big man in the small window, that's the one he prefers. The week before we had gone to Monsieur Béranger's and he hadn't liked his waffles, he hadn't liked them nor Monsieur Béranger, because of the way Monsieur Béranger looked at him, even though Dad didn't know, at first, that Monsieur Béranger was called Monsieur Béranger. When we had left his cafeteria, Dad had told us "I don't like him."

"Who?", we had asked.

"The guy."

"What guy?"

"The owner, the guy always chatting at the counter."

"Monsieur Béranger?"

"Might be."

"Might be what?"

"Might be Monsieur Béranger."

"But it's really Monsieur Béranger, it's true. That's his name."

"Yes, yes, but I didn't know that."

"What didn't you know?"

"That he was called Monsieur Béranger."

"And now, do you know it now?"

"Yes, now I do. But I didn't before."

"Before what?"

"Before you told me he's called Monsieur Béranger."

"So, what did you know before?"

"I knew I didn't like his waffles."

"Whose waffles?"

"Monsieur Béranger's."

"But if you didn't know he was Monsieur Béranger, then how could you have known you didn't like his waffles?"

"I knew I didn't like the waffles, even though I didn't know his name."

"You knew you didn't like Monsieur Béranger's waffles before you knew he was Monsieur Béranger?"

"Yes, I knew it."

"And now that you know he's Monsieur Béranger, do you like his waffles?"

"No, I still don't like his waffles nor his face. I don't like the way he looked at me."

"And how did he look at you?"

"Like this", Dad had said, stopping on the sidewalk in front of Monsieur Béranger's establishment and looking us in the eyes. We hadn't noticed anything besides his usual eyes and eyebrows. He had stared at us for a while, then cleared his throat, we had moved onwards.

At 10.14 a.m. Dad got up and went to the toilet, Bruce stated to both detectives. Alexei didn't like his waffle, which had some strawberries on top. The waitress brought it after Dad had gone to the toilet. She put it on our table and went away. She left, on the table, the waffle which Alexei didn't like. And we whispered to ourselves that he didn't like the waffle nor the topping, he didn't like the waffle itself nor the topping, the strawberries, in this case, that's what we said to ourselves, Dad couldn't hear us. Alexei chewed only one fork full of waffle and didn't swallow all of that fork full of waffle. While Dad went to the toilet, he spat out half the waffle, our Alexei spat out at least half the waffle he had put in his mouth, there was still another half of it in his mouth, the half he'd spit out was on his plate. Some saliva had reached me, I was quite close to him, I saw it flying in my direction. Then Alexei covered the half fork of spat-out waffle with a paper napkin, pushed the plate away from him and we were alone and quiet in our booth.

We heard Dad talking to someone behind us, not exactly behind us, but a bit farther away. So, as we were alone, Bruce said in the interrogation room, Alexei opened me up, he pulled open my zipper and stuffed me with his waffle, not all of it, because he had taken a full fork of it, half the forkful he had spit out, half he had left on his plate and, furthermore, he had cut a thin strip of waffle before sticking his fork in the remaining bigger chunk of waffle and stuffing it inside me together with some strawberries and a little bit of a gooey sauce.

Dad came to our booth, he sat down. He came back so soon Alexei didn't have the time to absorb some of the oil or fat or sauce or goo from the waffle, but maybe he didn't have the time and didn't think about it anyhow, or maybe he didn't have the time or he didn't think about it. Nevertheless, I tried to believe he had thought about it and simply hadn't had the time to act, for, with that intention in mind, I kept appreciating his gesture. At his age, intentions are all that count. From kids his age one cannot ask for results, only intentions, thus I felt uncomfortable and at the same time quite pleased with his care. Dad sat down opposite us. It was 10.20 a.m., gentlemen.

"You already ate the pancake? That was fast."

"It was a waffle, Dad, not a pancake", we said.

"Yes, waffle…", Dad looked down. "Waffle… pancake… I don't care if it was a waffle or a pancake. Did you eat it?", and he looked up.

"Yes", said our Alexei.

"You usually take a long time to eat. Did you really finish the pancake?"

"It wasn't a pancake."

"I don't care! From now on, I'm going to call it a pancake. Everything is a pancake. Even this table can be a pancake", Dad banged his fist on the table. "I'm paying the bill, I decide."

"But it was a waffle."

"I'm paying, I'm the payer! It was a pancake."

"But…"

"In my childhood, I didn't have pancakes nor waffles. I didn't have your opportunities as a kid."

"You didn't?"

"No, I didn't. Yet I succeeded."

"You did?"

Dad then said something I couldn't understand, Bruce the donkey confessed, he couldn't understand what his Dad had said. Bruce resumed speaking: Our Alexei nodded, Dad stopped talking, he looked at us after looking through the cafeteria's window, then back at us, again through the window, at us once more.

"You're still going around with that doll", Dad said.

"It's not a doll", our Alexei replied.

"Don't correct me."

"But it's not a doll."

"Dolls… waffles…"

And now Dad was hysterical, or nervous.

"Now I'm nervous, you see?", he said.

He banged his fist on the table, once again.

"I decide what's what, I'm your father. So, if I tell you it's a pancake, you can at least accept it to be pancake."

"But I told you…"

"Enough with your waffles!", he snapped. "You think you know everything because you're in school? I was once in school, too, I was, and I tell you, you don't learn everything in school."

For Dad, who had studied at school and even at university, one couldn't learn everything in school, just some things. School could undoubtedly be useful, but only for a part of life and certain matters and problems, never for everything, and Dad couldn't understand how our Alexei could believe that one can learn everything in school. According to Dad, some of the *stupidest people in the world* had frequented school and had also, most of them, gotten *university degrees*.

For Dad, completing school and graduating university did not equal either intellectual capacities or wisdom, and one must be mentally ill to believe otherwise. For Dad, one couldn't be mentally fit if one believed that frequenting school was enough to learn everything. In that case, one should be considered mentally impaired for life. And if he told us a waffle was a pancake, why shouldn't a waffle be a pancake? Anyway, Bruce admitted, I was eager to ask Dad whether a waffle should, from then on, always be considered a pancake, or whether only *that waffle* should be called a pancake. Despite my most humble wish, I remained silent.

Then Dad called the waitress, he waved at her, asked if she was leaving work late. She looked askance at him, moved away, taking a step to his left. Dad insisted, and while he was insisting, I was nevertheless feeling moist and greasy. I was indeed feeling greasy and moist inside, not all inside me, since that's impossible, all liquids suffer losses while being transferred from one recipient to another… minor losses in pipe flow; minor losses; friction losses; total head loss… But my central axis and matrix were being affected, the grease was reaching my nuclear sensors. It might be reaching my neck, but we couldn't see whether it was reaching my neck or not, neither of us, neither our Alexei nor me.

Dad insisted on asking the waitress what time she was getting off, again she didn't answer, Dad blinked at her several times, he almost seemed to have some foreign object in his eye, a mosquito in this eye, a hair, a beard hair which might have travelled from his chin or cheeks to his eye, he blinked and at last he shrugged. Alexei slid across the bench, he stopped in front of me.

"Bring us another pancake, please. Quickly, I must go and work, ok?", Dad said.

"A pancake? It might take a few extra minutes, sir", the waitress finally spoke and thus answered Dad's request.

"So what? It always takes a few minutes, the pancake", Dad argued.

"At least a few more minutes than the waffle you just ordered, sir, that's what I meant."

"You meant what?", Dad pointed to Alexei's plate. "I want this pancake here", he pointed once more, but there was no pancake nor waffle there, the plate was clear of pancakes and waffles, though greasy or gooey with remnants of strawberries. Alexei was chewing on a bit of strawberry. In fact, gentlemen, and please accept my apologies, there was a tiny bit of waffle on the plate, as there lay the half forkful of waffle our Alexei had spit out. "The one he ate."

"Yes, you want a waffle", the waitress said.

"I call it a pancake. But… it doesn't matter."

"It doesn't matter?"

"No, it doesn't matter."

"But you want a waffle, not a pancake, right?"

"I told you I want a pancake. Don't you understand what I'm saying?"

"I understood you said you wanted a pancake, that's what I heard, but then you seemed to be ordering a waffle."

"Yes, I want a pancake, that's it. Like the one the kid ate, and like the one I ate."

"He ate a waffle", the waitress said, though Alexei hadn't *de facto* eaten a waffle, but at most only a tiny bit of waffle.

"But I can call it a pancake, can't I? Is that hard to understand?"

"No."

"No what?"

"It's not hard to understand."

"So, there you see."

"But he didn't eat a pancake. It was a waffle, whatever you want to call it."

"Are we living in a free country, or what?" Dad said, banging his fist on the table.

The waitress hushed Dad, she asked him to be quiet, "Be quiet, please", she said, and asked him to calm down, "Calm down", she said. If he wouldn't calm down and stop annoying the other clients, she wouldn't bring him a new waffle, or a waffle or a pancake or anything else, instead, she would call the police. First, she would call the manager, then the manager would call the police. No waffles, no pancakes. The waitress went away. Dad calmed down, he crossed his fingers on the table and stared straight ahead, with his hands entwined he looked straight ahead and then at Alexei. A moment later he looked straight ahead and at us, after that only at us.

"You all think you're better than me. But I went to school, too, you know."

"I know, Dad", we answered.

"And to university. I was a genius."

"Yes, Dad."

Dad sighed, looked at me, sighed again, looked down, then at me, and said: "Do you always bring that doll with you?"

"Not always", Alexei replied.

"You spend too much money on batteries."

"Not really."

"No? I bet you're always turning it on."

"Sometimes, yes."

"So, you do waste batteries, and then spend your money on batteries, of course."

"Andrei and Babushka give me some money for batteries, so I don't spend my money."

"Good… But you do spend their money…"

"Yes, they give me some money, I spend it on batteries."

"They have some money, yes", Dad rolled his eyes and leaned towards me over the table. Then he sniffed the air, enlarged his nostrils, and almost touched me with the tip of his nose.

"It's disgusting. This doll smells like grease."

Alexei got closer. He too sniffed the air.

"Can't smell anything, Dad."

"You should get rid of it, instead of wasting batteries. You'll be my ruin. You and your doll. That was my biggest mistake ever."

Dad stood up from the chair, cleared his throat and walked away towards the counter. He turned around, told us to stay put, because he was going to pay the bill. The waitress hadn't yet brought another waffle, but he was going to pay, he said, so we should keep quiet. At the counter, he called the waitress, she was talking to an old lady at some distance. She didn't look at him, and Dad called her again. She did not reply and continued to talk to the old woman. A gentleman approached Dad from the other side of the counter, he said something, but Dad didn't reply. When the waitress came back from the old lady's table, approaching Dad, Alexei touched me, his hand under my nose then on my belly, after that in my belly, his fingers touching the core, my metallic core, gentlemen, touch it and you will find it cold, I myself can't feel the cold as it is part of me, and actually it isn't cold at all, but made of conductor material, thus having no heat source around it, my core seems to be cold to other people, they often touch it and say it's cold, or better still, they often say it's cold whenever they happen to touch it, though they seldom do touch it. I myself don't feel the coldness of my core, though I did feel his fingers. Alexei was pulling fragments of waffle out of me, including the half-fork of waffle he had spit out. He then threw them to the floor. Dad came back, sat down and stared at us. The waitress showed up with a waffle.

"Here you go", she said, leaving a plate on the table.

"Miss, please…", Dad beseeched.

She left. Suddenly Dad reached us over the table, he touched my head, my core, he fumbled inside me.

"It's all greasy!", he said.

We asked him what he was doing, he told us he wanted to find the button. We wondered what button, and presently Alexei wondered what button it was, but we two stopped wondering as I felt and knew it was my on/off button.

We went out.

Alexei was holding me, his fingers still inside my fabric, touching my core, one finger almost on the button. Dad stood beside us. He tried to grab me, we moved away, one, two, three, four steps, there was light, sunbeams between the clouds, Dad's face illuminated, it might have been beautiful, dear gentlemen, I don't know if I'm allowed to delve into aesthetics, perhaps it would take up too much time, Bruce the plush donkey said to both detectives. We lost our balance, we three, and I fell on the pavement. Face down, I could see the cement, grey with tiny grains of sand, Bruce said. The coldness of the cement I couldn't sense, as contrary to my core my external fabric lacks all sensibility, gentlemen, I could not feel the cold concrete nor would I feel your hands twisting my arms, nor a flame burning my tail, though I could eventually feel your hands twisting my arms or a flame burning my tail due to preestablished human concepts, dear gentlemen, but then:

"Turn it off."

"No. No, stop."

Then I saw the sky, the pavement again, the sky, some trees with red leaves, the sky, the pavement, I stopped moving.

"No", Alexei said, followed by footsteps. I distanced myself from the cement, I saw buildings, cars, the sky. "He's going to get dirty."

Dad approached us and snorted. Alexei tried to get rid of the dirt, he tried to clean me.

"I'm off to work", Dad said.

"Can I come, too, and watch?", we asked.

"You can."

Dad grumbled over and over, he couldn't stop grumbling while he walked, and we followed him.

We went onward, it was 10.56 a.m., Dad crossed the street at 10.56 a.m., we walked behind him, we entered Dad's workplace, his office, as he calls it, come on, come in and don't touch anything in the office, Dad said, he always tells us to enter the office and beware, clean your shoes before entering the office, and often he says don't touch anything you pigheaded dork, respect my office, though, in fact, it is more a workshop than an office, dear gentlemen. To be honest, it's not an office at all, only a dusty and straightforward workshop, one accesses it through a rolling door, it's a garage door, or a garage-like door, a deposit room door,

it opens to the street, Dad rolls it up, it rolls itself up in red-painted metal sheets. We entered
the workshop at 10.59 a.m., Dad coughed,
dragged us inside, pulled us by our arms, he
rolled down the metallic door, then switched on
the light.

10.59 a.m

Gentlemen, you keep asking me to hurry up and get to the point, but I am indeed getting to the point, in a fairy tale one begins with once upon a time, but there's no beginning and no end in my story, one could almost say my story is a sphere, a perfect round sphere, no angles, no edges, there are no points one must delve into before delving into other points, or maybe there are, but the fact is that at 10.59 a.m. Dad was supposedly in an unknown location, though in his workshop, while Babushka was at home, or presumably at home. She used to have a hard time breathing, so I guess she was at home at 10.59 a.m. that day, and mostly every day, to be honest, Bruce the plush donkey said. I believe she was indeed at home that morning, since she had problems breathing, she couldn't handle everyday life as she should, all because breathing was so difficult for her, and that's why we don't like our older brother Andrei to smoke inside the house and we tell him to do it outside, but he just laughs at us and ask us to close the windows, because it's very cold out in autumn and winter and we don't want any draughts inside, and in summer it's too hot and the heat comes inside along with the mosquitoes, and then we must shut the windows. Andrei keeps smoking indoors and the smoke lingers in the air. "This stuff helps her breathe, it has therapeutic properties," he said one day, "But good or bad properties?", we asked, "Good", he answered. Then we left his room and went to ours and left it too and entered the living room and counted five minutes on the clock and went back to his room. He was still smoking. "And now, has the smoke good or bad properties?", we asked. "Good. Go away!" he replied, and we opened the two windows once we were again in the living room. Since the smell of smoke gets stuck on clothes, we should open the windows more often, and we should also freshen up the air to kill the dust mites, to remove the smell of smoke and kill the dust mites. Our Alexei saw some pictures of dust mites in school, I was at home, and the pictures were taken with a microscope, the microscope enlarged the tiny creatures and helped our Alexei to see what they look like, later he told us what he had seen, I didn't see them, I was at home with Babushka, our Alexei left me in our room, I could only hear Babushka coughing, sneezing and grabbing pots and pans in the kitchen, then Alexei arriving, all morning and afternoon I heard Babushka wheezing, coughing, sneezing and grabbing pots and pans, turning on the faucet, when she turned on the faucet I couldn't hear her wheezing, or I listened to a bit of coughing and wheezing, and turning on the faucet only dampened the noise. She sounded like a rabbit coughing. When Alexei took me to a pet shop, I heard a rabbit coughing, then we got home and asked Babushka if she knew about rabbits coughing, because our young Babushka used to have rabbits, she once lived in Russia, and she had rabbits.

"I had rabbits in Russia, and sometimes some of them would start to cough and wheeze, and then they died", and on the first occasion we heard her tell us about the rabbits our Alexei asked her if they buried the rabbits that died. Babushka told us they ate the rabbits that died, whether from coughing and wheezing or from getting a punch in the neck, just behind the head, a stroke with an axe or a punch with a clenched fist, they would eat them anyway, and then Alexei didn't ask about it ever again. Babushka would tell us about the rabbits and how her parents gave them grass and cabbage to eat, and he wouldn't ask about them being buried, though I wished he would ask her, I certainly could ask about it myself, but then Babushka might get confused seeing me speak, Bruce admitted to the two detectives, and at her age this kind of confusion can get a person sent to the asylum, some people land in the asylum for getting confused in old age, truth be told, that happens quite often, like Madame Feodorovna's husband's sister, she and her husband took her to an asylum for demented people in Sorel-Tracy, our Alexei and I went with them all the way up there, Madame Feodorovna's husband drove and we sat next to his sister, who is demented and even confused. The asylum looked nice and clean, dear gentlemen, but Sorel-Tracy is not reachable on foot for people like our Alexei and me, so we want to avoid any kind of visiting in Sorel-Tracy, and thus keep Babushka home, perhaps try and convince Monsieur Pereira to let us use a tiny part of his backyard and there, in that tiny part of his backyard, build a rabbit-house for a rabbit or two, we can either have one rabbit or two, we must ponder this possibility, as it may be preferable to start off with one rabbit and only later get another rabbit to keep him or her company, for one can start with one rabbit and then get another one to make them two rabbits, nevertheless one cannot start off with two rabbits and all of sudden have only one rabbit in the rabbit-house, unless one disposes of the rabbit, by selling him or her, killing him or her, or throwing him or her above the backyard fence, and all these possibilities seem quite unnecessary and uncomfortable for one of the rabbits, namely the one we would have to sell, kill or throw above the backyard fence, and even unfair if one takes into account how this issue could be solved by getting, at first, only one rabbit instead of two.

Anyway, we still need to approach this matter with Monsieur Pereira, as we haven't in fact done so yet. The closest we have gotten to mention this idea of building a rabbit-house in Monsieur Pereira's backyard to him was when we stopped in front of a store and out of it came Monsieur Pereira, he said hello to Babushka, and we said hello to Monsieur Pereira, Babushka was not coughing and wheezing, but speaking freely and with ease, walking a little bit outdoors for hygienic reasons. She asked Monsieur Pereira if he had a rabbit on his sweater. She pointed to Monsieur Pereira's sweater and asked if it was a rabbit on his sweater, a white rabbit with long ears, and Monsieur Pereira answered yes, madam, it's a rabbit, he said while opening up his jacket, with both hands he pulled his jacket's sides to the left and right showing the rabbit on his sweater.

"Do you like it, madam?"

"Yes, I do. I had rabbits in Russia", she said, though, in fact, the rabbits were not hers, but her parents'. Dear gentlemen, she said she had rabbits but didn't say they were her parents'. We knew it because she had said it before, so we knew they were her parents' when we found Monsieur Pereira leaving the store, it wasn't our Dad's store.

Dad rolled down his workshop's metallic door, he covered the front window. We became surrounded by darkness, it was all around us, no rays of light entering his workshop. He turned the light on, we heard him touching the switch, after that we saw electronic equipment and wires and cables and tools. I was born there, only me, not our Alexei, he was born in a hospital, Alexei had me in his arms when we entered the workshop, Bruce said while sitting before two police detectives, proceeding to describe with accuracy all the actions and reactions previous to his witnessing of a murder, a hideous crime, as a woman had been killed in a building on the other side of the street from where Bruce dwelled, a woman in her 30's, as one newspaper would erroneously call her, a woman in her 30's but who was indeed 29, had been killed a few days before in her apartment, the police had no suspects yet. Our Dad walked to a counter and grabbed a wrench, then a hammer, dropped the wrench and started immediately to beat on some pieces of steel on the bench. Our Alexei walked around, Bruce told the detectives, and he could sense they were annoyed. Sometimes I think my burden is to annoy people *when I want only to enlighten them*, he said, afterwards, in regard to his interrogation by the police. I gazed at them and clearly saw they were despising me and had difficulties in believing me, for I am a thinking and talking plush donkey, he later told Alexei. For them, I was doubtlessly an aberration, because I am a plush donkey that can think and speak like one of them, as a detective and as a *human being*, he said. They were probably both disgusted at questioning and listening to a stuffed donkey that thought and spoke like or *even better* than them. Perhaps they would not loathe me so much were I to think and speak like an idiot, i.e., like one of them, or worse than an idiot, i.e., like one of them, but they most surely could not stand to question and listen to a plush donkey that in truth thought and spoke better than them, he said. He could almost imagine what they were thinking about, but not really, and he couldn't stop wondering what it might be they were thinking about… where's this little freak going with this, thought one of the policemen, the one on the right, Detective Mercier, who supported himself on the desk, sighed, looked over his partner's shoulder, there were tiny flocks of dandruff all over his blazer. Damn cuck this asshole's loathsome he can't wash his head if he properly washed his head he would have a chance with his sweetheart or maybe not I'm much more handsome than him goddamn cuckold I like his sheets though I wonder where he bought them they're so soft I would purchase those sheets need to ask his wife where they bought them but maybe they also need to be washed with a specific detergent Emma can't do the washing stupid fat whore she could get together with this asshole he and his dandruff and she with her poorly washed bed linen just look at these shoulders what a mess and he can't even make an inquiry why are we looking at this stuffed donkey it's ridiculous I should intervene call the press yes that's what I should do call the media and blow up all this nonsense someone's playing us someone's pulling our leg both our legs and we can't walk anymore we move in circles sitting in office chairs this dandruff mountain can't even see anything an explosion of dandruff a pile of white flecks next time I'll meet his wife right in front of him let's invite them to dinner that fat bastardly stinking cow of my wife can prepare us a meal while I grab his wife's thighs under the table pinching her soft flesh, thus thought one of the policemen, Detective Mercier, he's the one who preferred to stand while his mate was writing something with a pen and Bruce the little plush donkey was talking about his Dad. At 11.04 a.m. the phone in the workshop rang.

"Pick up the phone", Dad said to us. Alexei searched for it and found the phone under the worktop. It rang again. "Pick it up!" Dad insisted, he was starting to feel nervous. "The phone is starting to make me nervous", he said.

Alexei picked up the phone with one hand, still grabbing me with the other, it was a lady asking for Dad, she wanted to have a washing machine repaired. Dad sighed. "A man of my intrinsic value thus reduced to abjection!", he said, as he used to say, but he didn't pick up the phone himself. Our Alexei continued to talk to the lady, he's talented, can speak with ladies, young and old, especially with Babushka, he calls her sometimes when we're far away. She seldom picks up the phone, gentlemen, she's usually sleeping or stretching her back on the couch, and mostly coughing. Dad says she heats our apartment too much, but maybe it's because Andrei doesn't allow us to open the windows.

Now a synapsis made the detective called Anderson jump out of his chair, he woke up as soon as he heard Bruce talking about windows: You were sitting on a windowsill when the crime occurred, right?, Detective Anderson, sitting and jotting down notes, asked. The crime, so, you mean the murder, Bruce said. Detective Anderson, still jotting down notes and sitting opposite Bruce, folded a paper and reflected. Just a little bit. What will she cook for dinner I'm starving it would be nice to have dinner in a restaurant once in a while maybe I could read a bit over there at the restaurant carefully, don't want to smudge the book cover with grease stains why did I stain the other books it's always the book I like the most never the ones I sell her potato salad is killing me my stomach hurts I get cramps can't think about it now or I'll begin to retch maybe I could stop by a restaurant and have a light meal before going home yes but then I would have to eat her food anyway I hope she's not home, thus reflected Detective Anderson, who had begun to read Descartes's works and works on Descartes's works the day before, but he didn't reach any conclusion. Yes, I was sitting on a windowsill, it's true, Bruce the stuffed donkey admitted. Anyway, he got back to what he was talking about.

So, gentlemen, Dad told us to note down the client's address, "Note down the client's address", he said. He was referring to the lady who called, our Dad, I mean. Our Dad was. Our Alexei asked the lady client's address, he looked for a pen and a piece of paper, though it was unnecessary, I could have told them the lady client's address if they told me the lady client's address too, or to be precise, later I could have told them the lady client's address if they had told me her address beforehand, that way I could memorize it. They didn't tell me the lady client's address. Alexei found a pen and a scrap of paper, he then put me down on the worktop, grabbed the phone again and wrote something on the dirty piece of paper, I could hear Dad banging on something, a metallic sound. Alexei hung up at 11.07 a.m.

A link? Yes, between the call and the crime, asked Detective Anderson. Monsieur Detective, I can't tell you there's a link between this lady's call and the murdered woman, there might be a link, you're the detective, please edify me. And would you be so kind as to turn my neck a little bit, sir, please, I'm now staring in part at the floor, as you may see for yourself, please adjust my position, Monsieur Detective, dear gentlemen, one of you may help me without even straining your muscles too much. Thank you. On the windowsill, I was sitting up straight, as you can see my core is quite hard and sustains my loose parts if one takes the time to put me down in an adequate way, not in a wrong way, I don't go as far as to call it a *wrong way,* but, in a sense, yes, there's a wrong and right or proper way of leaving me be. Babushka was somewhere in the apartment; I heard her wheezing and snoring afterwards. She was snoring when the man entered the living room on the other side of the street. The front building is red, you know, made of red-orange bricks, there are trees in between, our Alexei would arrive later, he would enter his bedroom and leave his bedroom, I know because I would hear him coming in and out of his room, a floorboard in the doorway of his room creaks whenever someone steps on it, it creaked and creaked again.

"The stairs smell like grilled meat", our Alexei then said to Babushka, and I got a whiff from his clothes, it could be grilled meat, or charred potatoes, too, and sometimes I feel happy because Dad has made me as I am, for he has built me with a sense of vision and a sense of hearing and a sense of smell and some sense of feeling around my core, and some other times I think *I should* feel unhappy, since there are foul smells, at least they are considered foul odours, nevertheless, I can smell manure, for instance, and not feel the slightest bit nauseated or repulsed, for I am not a biological entity. Therefore, I lack any need to avoid certain smells or sources of smells, as nature does not need to teach me not to eat manure, because I can't eat, but then one has a lot of social knowledge and learning attached to his personality and mind, and people say manure stinks and I learn that manure stinks and that's it, in my brain the smell of manure gets associated with stink and repulsion. To be honest, some people like manure and its smell. Monsieur Pereira has flowerpots and flowerbeds in his backyard, and he uses manure to make the flowers bloom, his wife often comes along to contemplate the beautiful blossoms, we see them from our windows, Babushka stares at the flowers and so do we, yellow and white and red and violet flowers, Monsieur Pereira spreads the manure over the soil, he reaches inside some plastic bags, takes handfuls of manure out of them and then spreads the manure with his little hoe, Babushka tells us to close the windows, we close the windows, at least when Andrei is not home and the windows are open, "Close the windows, Alexei", she says, "or the rooms will start to stink", and we close the windows, if they're not already closed, because she may say this when they are open but also when they're closed. Monsieur Pereira continues to spread manure, and he tells his wife that's some good manure, we think he says it even when we close our windows. Once Alexei opened one window and waved to Monsieur Pereira, he was talking to his wife, and then we asked him how he was, and he said he was fine, and that that manure was good, excellent in truth. "I have dealt with manure for decades, but this is some of the best I've ever touched. I was telling my wife it's some excellent manure, it's horse manure", and every time we see him in the backyard talking to his wife while spreading manure, he opens his arms and points to the tiny piles of manure around the flowerbeds, he must be telling her about the quality of manure, he grabs handfuls of it, and she listens, sometimes I try to open the window to listen, too. It's actually just a wish, I can't open the window. Those windows are the back windows, turned to the backyard, the building where the man perpetrated the crime is located on the other side, the front windows faced towards it. It was in the afternoon, our Alexei wasn't home yet, only Babushka and me. Later, when Alexei arrived, he complained about the stench in the stairs, and said the postman had left a letter for Babushka under the doormat, and it was probably lying under the doormat since the day before, as they don't deliver post on Saturdays, so the letter must have been lying there since the day before, Friday, or the day before that, Thursday, but possibly not since Wednesday, for we had vacuumed the flat and the doormat on Wednesday, we and Andrei together. Well, we were appalled by that lazy postal service, as the letter could have gotten trampled on or wet or stolen by the upstairs neighbour, but thankfully Alexei picked it up. When he opened the door, he felt the silence, and he knew Andrei was not at home, because there was no smoke and no loud music, Andrei was working, he works part-time in a pizza store.

"Who's there?"

"I'm home, Babushka", said our Alexei.

Babushka could barely speak. She coughed. It seemed she would never stop coughing. It was a long, drawn, loud and endless cough. Alexei went into our room and entered the little living room where Babushka was sitting on the couch, sunk in her convulsive lungs. I remained on the windowsill.

"Babushka, do you want something for your cough?" he asked.

"I have to pick up Andrei and bring him home."

"Where from?"

"From school, of course. He never pays attention when crossing the street, you know."

Babushka was lost in her mind, once again senile. Alexei filled a glass of water in the kitchen, I heard him turning on the faucet, I was still looking at the front building, the woman's corpse was lying there on the second floor, my back was turned to our living room, I then heard Alexei spill some water, "Damn", he said, "Don't swear, Alexei", Babushka said, and she coughed, he spilled some water because his hands shook. "I spilled some water, my hands are shaking", he added. Babushka could rest while she was sitting, and Alexei should rest, too, it tires him to stand up and walk, hold the glass, fix her dentures and so on, she looks like a shrivelled prune, she's an invalid, she was once only a bit of an invalid, only an invalid when she arrived home in the evening, though not at all in the mornings, she's always been a morning rose and very much appreciated going out, maybe she sang while walking to work, I think she did so.

"Do you remember when you used to work?", we asked her.

"Oh, I do."

"You woke up very early, didn't you, Babushka?"

"Yes… I think so."

"What time did you get out of bed in the morning?"

"I don't know exactly."

"Around 6, wasn't it?"

"Maybe."

"Yes, it was, most times it wasn't even daylight, right?"

"No daylight at all, to work hard, one must wake up early, before sunrise."

"And you could breathe and walk normally, couldn't you, Babushka? You felt good."

"Those were the times, my dear."

"Yes, they were."

I thought about asking her what time she used to arrive home, but Alexei shut up and stayed silent. Then nothing happened, and Alexei turned on the television.

"Babushka, the postman left a letter at the door", he said, in the opposite building blood had stained the floorboards, namely in the flat I had seen a man attacking a woman.

"Well, I thought I had heard someone knocking", Babushka said.

Babushka isn't deaf, but her brain is getting lazier and lazier. She's not yet as Madame Feodorovna, she's a chucklehead, and she leaks a bit. Babushka also fears she might start to leak and get wet.

"Do you want me to read it for you?", our Alexei asked.

He read the letter. They were calling Babushka to the hospital because of her lungs. She must be there tomorrow, dear gentleman, yes, tomorrow.

"On the 29th? What day is that?"

Babushka sounded scared. Why?, I thought whilst looking out the window, my back turned to the living room. Was she afraid of going to the hospital alone? I could keep her company. But she was, as it happens, afraid of undressing herself and not being clean enough. Ever since we learned that Madame Feodorovna leaks, Babushka fears losing some drops, "I fear losing some drops of urine", she says occasionally, and the woman's corpse had leaked and was still leaking, too, in her case, blood, for she was dead. In fact, I am only stating an assumption, my conviction that the woman was dead. Although I *now* know that she was indeed dead, *then* I wasn't sure she was dead. I suspected she was dead, but I wasn't sure she was, and even though I now know that she died, that doesn't allow me to ascertain she was *already* dead, as I don't know at which moment her death occurred — she may have died minutes later, not being dead yet when our Alexei spilled some water on the floor and Babushka arguably feared she might leak in the hospital. "I might leak in the hospital", she stated. Our Alexei and I heard Babushka, he approached her, I heard his steps getting closer, "You don't leak, Babushka", he said, I remained on the windowsill, in the opposite block of flats the blood had spread over the floor, and the man I had seen earlier had left, he had crossed the living room, turned around, looked at the floor, seemed to say something, he had moved his lips, I presume he said something, perhaps he swore, he had bent down and looked attentively to the floor, then he had straightened himself, turned one shoe over, taken a look at its sole, the second shoe had followed suit, he supported himself on only one foot while doing this, he had turned around again, moved across the room, disappeared behind the door.

Babushka was trying to get up, I heard her efforts when she raised herself on an elbow, it's always the same, the sofa screeches, she coughs. Alexei was holding her free hand; I had my back turned on them but could see everything in my mind's eye. Then the phone rang, Alexei picked it up as he had picked up the phone in Dad's workshop, where our Alexei had hung up on that lady client at 11.07 a.m.

Dad grabbed the telephone, he simply clutched it once our Alexei hung up, I should say with violence, or should I refrain from stating the obvious, is it obvious?, Bruce the plush donkey thought to himself, I don't know if it's obvious, gentlemen, he said to both detectives, but Dad picked up the telephone from the table, Bruce said, he grabbed it and threw it against the wall in a fit of rage. Our Alexei sighed, then spoke. "What did you do that for?", he asked. "I felt like it", Dad said, "I'm furious." But then he said no more, he didn't explain why he was mad, he told the detectives. Dad didn't say anything more, if only for half a minute.

"I! Me! A man like me reduced to fixing washing machines!", he cried.

"A man like you?", we asked.

"Yes, a man like me."

"How is it a man like you, Dad?"

"Well, you know… a smart man. A man like me… how do you say it in French… a man with many skills!"

"Skills, Dad?"

"Yes, a genius. You know, the KGB wanted…"

"You had many skills the KGB was looking for?"

"Yes, and I still have them. It's unfair! If I were an American engineer…", Dad said, and he pounded his fist on the counter, he seemed enraged, Bruce told the detectives, he was feeling immensely bored, perhaps there's an inner violence in all men all human beings I am no human being and can't feel it I don't have it in me my core is a cold piece of metal filled with wires chips and batteries Dad granted me the capacity to think and understand human speech to see and hear and smell my wires connected to eyes and ears and a nose Dad was capable of building such a machine in the mid-90's it's a miracle of science and engineering now that's pure Russian intellect put to use… yes I doubt an American could do it come on just between us that's the truth anyway nevertheless just look at these two both Canadian citizens yet dumb as dumb can be well I assume both of them are Canadian otherwise they wouldn't be police in

Canada that's legally impossible as is my understanding of how things work regarding authorities yes at least as far as I know they couldn't be police unless they are Canadian at least I don't think they're American perhaps they hate me to their guts because they're American everyone's well aware of how Americans despise Canadians I won't say all Americans despise Canadians and Canada but many of them do they say we're pussies or that *you* are pussies probably I'm not considered a Canadian I have no citizenship I shouldn't be so full of myself to the point of believing Americans would think about me as a Canadian citizen or that they think about me *at all* no I am barely noticeable these two detectives can look at me without really seeing me not even my fellow Canadian neighbours notice my presence in this country named Canada namely in the beautiful city of Montreal… in this country I live surrounded by Canadians but not only Canadians there are also Americans… those Americans attacked Mother Russia… Dad was unfairly treated… a man with his skills… yes there are Americans among us those despicable Americans more often found south of Canada oh Canadaaaaa you're smiling

is it am I a joke to you dear gentlemen now
that's silly of me they can't hear you thinking
Bruce stop with this foolishness they're just
dumb like Americans well the Americans let's
not speak badly about them a few might feel offended or some might feel offended or many
might be offended though it's nearly impossible
that all or none might be offended with my
ideas about Americans and even shocked to
know what I think about Americans if they ever
get access to my records my internal records recording recording everything must be recorded
but this is only a stupid plush donkey thinking
that's a good important piece of information to
record too let's not make a fuss about my ideas
and in Montreal there's plenty of people to despise in Montreal one can find people from anywhere in the world including Portugal just like
the aforementioned Monsieur Pereira and Portuguese are much worse than Americans they're
dirty stupid low-life scumbags I bet the woman
was murdered by a Portuguese criminal he
surely could be a Portuguese schizophrenic moronic piece of trash I can't say I saw him clearly
but he could definitely be a Portuguese anthro-

pological failure as all Portuguese are to be Portuguese is to be a creep a jagged double-faced hypocrite like that man who kicked me when my Alexei dropped me poor Alexei the guy kicked me and swore in Portuguese couldn't he be a Portuguese it's possible though improbable, thought Bruce, one swears in his mother language one always swears and calls for god or mommy in his native language it's all explicitly described in literature cinema art history books he kicked me and swore in Portuguese poor Alexei he didn't know what to say he didn't even know the man had spoken Portuguese that guy was a scumbag this is true for that asshole but also applies to all of them with a few exceptions only a quite limited number of exceptions such as the Portuguese readers who may read any of my eventual future books yes any of my novels-to-be I hope I can get them published my ideas are manifold I even share some with our neighbour and friend Michel he too wants to write novels one day it seems it's funny that he too wants to write everyone wants to write and no one wants to read indeed yes well I do have many ideas need to ask my Alexei to note them down and then write them the ideal would be to request Dad to add some kind of plug-in to me and connect me directly to one of these new computers then I could process text immediately anyway I have to get those novels written so I shall exclude at least all the potential Portuguese readers of my books who won't hate them and speak critically about them but let's exclude all the Portuguese readers who won't speak badly about my books even if they don't enjoy them yes those readers and a few more Portuguese these are or might be good people and Monsieur Pereira and his wife too but not that Portuguese guy who kicked me he's another piece of shit maybe it was him who killed the woman.

You know, the killer may be a Portuguese man, Bruce told the detectives, who both pricked their ears, though Anderson more than Mercier, for the latter was feeling sweaty and a painful stinging in his abdomen, I saw a medium-height man with brown hair crossing the living room in the block of flats opposite our own flat, this is the beginning of a physical description, therefore an important matter, please write down some notes, dear gentlemen, and Anderson jotted down a few words, *description:*

possible murderer, Bruce resumed speaking a minute later. Though, to be honest, Bruce said, this is not a good description of the murderer if the murderer is taken to be a Portuguese, yes, let's say the woman was killed by a Portuguese, so, referring to him as medium-height and brown-haired or chestnut-haired, probably with brown-hazel eyes is not exactly the best description possible, as that comprises most Portuguese people, at least most Portuguese people living abroad, like in Montreal's Portuguese neighbourhood, and I would go as far as to state it comprises most Portuguese people anywhere in the world, including their small country, just a slice of earth, a clot of dirt in Europe's ass, despite having only access, as a non-free moving plush donkey, to the Portuguese I have met in Montreal, as I have never left Montreal, dear gentlemen, I have nonetheless taken into account all empirical phenotypical information and encyclopaedic data I've gathered so far, so it's not far-fetched to assume most Portuguese, both by citizenship and genetics, and as such Portuguese citizens or barely genetically or ethnically Portuguese people, though mostly the genetically Portuguese, since a genetically non-

Portuguese could get to be a Portuguese citizen notwithstanding their hair and skin colour, thus one may conclude the most part of Portuguese are brunet, they have swarthy complexions, including dark hair, mainly brown in different hues several degrees of brown ranging from almost-black to almost-blond following the scale ranging between the darkest and the lightest brown, one can't exclude blonds and redheads, but it's probably fair to assume they're mostly brunet, anyway, I'm sorry for diverting from the main issue, dear gentlemen, but as you know, every single detail might be of importance, life and occurrences are a perfect sphere, no angles and no end, you are detectives and surely understand why I can't leave all the connecting dots and wires and cables and threads lying around out there untouched unseen unheard. In short, the man was of medium height and had brown hair, Bruce the donkey said, and Detective Anderson wrote it down.

"Please do describe more thoroughly the man you saw", Detective Anderson asked whilst sitting at the table, his pen in mid-air, his hand ready to write.

"What do you mean, dear Monsieur Detective?", Bruce asked.

"Detective Anderson, please."

Bruce didn't answer. He was taking his time reflecting.

"So?", the detective pressed on.

"So what?"

"Can you please tell us more about that guy?"

"Yes, I can."

Silence. Detective Anderson cleared his throat, Detective Mercier rose from his chair and started walking around the interrogation room, he looked nervous, was he thinking about his partner's wife?, perhaps, but then maybe not, no, he wasn't thinking about her at all, in fact he wasn't even thinking, he was feeling quite a strong abdominal pain, he feared it might be something conspicuous, a gaseous pain stretching his intestinal walls, intestines are our second brain, they contain precious immunity cells, intestines create a barrier, a block of glands and juices, membranes absorbing and secreting fluids, one can't easily break through intestinal walls, it's a well-known fact, as it is their importance, our second brain, our second

heart, my heart is where my intestines are, people are influenced by their intestines' health,
just like Detective Mercier, a true Québécoise,
his ancestors came all the way to Quebec from
Northern Paris, his intestines are genetically
French, a bit mixed up with other branches of
intestinification being mostly French, these
same intestines were now blocking all his hearing, Bruce the plush donkey was speaking, Mercier couldn't hear him, he glanced at him once
in a while, but as Bruce didn't move his lips and
tongue to communicate, Mercier wasn't sure if
he was speaking at all. Bruce didn't have lips in
the true sense, his lips were mere lines of
thread, sewed to his face, and he lacked a
tongue, there was nothing inside his mouth, behind those tight lips, the words he pronounced
came from a compact sound-surround system
implanted in his core, deep within him, so he
could be more easily heard when he was open,
his core accessible, his words spreading and
hovering in the air, his lips not moving, Mercier
traversed the interrogation room once again, he
rubbed his belly, he was starting to get paunchy,
he drank too much beer, he hit the bottle as
soon as he finished his shift, went to a fancy bar

downtown with other policemen, or crossed the city to less pretentious places, seedy bars with shoddy clientele, no women around, sometimes he met Evelyn, his friend the cuckhold's wife, now there's another name, this is getting tight, very tight, now we're reaching something, we might find out who killed the woman, Mercier's intestines might solve the case if they had legs and arms, and let's at least suppose the killer wasn't Evelyn, as the victim appears to have been killed by a *man*. Suddenly: god damnit, Mercier thought, yes, finally he began to think, there was an idea somewhere in that skull, under his pia mater, god damnit, fuck Anderson, he's a sack of dandruff. And then he rubbed his belly.

"Let's have a break", he suggested.

Anderson looked at him.

"Now?"

"Why not? The toy isn't talking, is it?"

"But…"

"This is stupid! I'm out."

Mercier was walking toward the door when Bruce said:

"Maybe there's a connection, I even thought about that when Dad picked the phone again and dialled a number at 11.11 a.m."

Mercier stopped at the door, what connection, he thought for a moment, then he rushed out of the room and into the corridor towards the toilets, leaving the interrogation room door open. Anderson rose from his chair to close the door, and so he did. He went back to the table, Bruce was sitting opposite him, the tape recorder was still on, Anderson sat down and sighed, he was taken by a sudden despondency, he could laugh at his partner for leaving the room in a hurry, with his hands on his belly, a liquidly gaseous sound reverberating in his abdomen, pushing perchance his diaphragm, yet he didn't laugh, he sat down and looked at Bruce, then at the tape recorder, he tapped his pen on the notebook, he didn't know why he felt so sad, there was no apparent reason to feel blue, anyway, he was sitting opposite a plush donkey, perhaps Mercier was right and someone was pulling their legs, he wanted to go home, that was it, Anderson envisioned himself resting on his couch, taking off his sweaty shirt, he was uncomfortable, now the donkey was speaking freely, what he had to say didn't cheer him up either, Bruce was delving into a possible connection to the KGB, as his Dad supposedly had been recruited by the KGB while still living in Ukraine, this had happened before the fall of the Soviet Union, of course, before all the surviving family had moved to Canada, Babushka and her daughter — Alexei's mother —, Dad and Andrei, a still-unborn Alexei, maybe he was in fact an already existing entity, an embryo conceived on Soviet soil, also escaping the atomic radiation that had killed Grandpa and made them flee from Pripyat, Dad had been contacted by the KGB way before the atomic incident in Chernobyl, Dad was a young engineer, and a quite talented one.

"Dad was learning English and French when he moved to Canada."

"What did you say?", Anderson asked.

But Anderson didn't really want to know what he had said, besides despondent he felt bored, he wanted to leave, too, like Mercier, maybe clean out his bowels, get rid of all the bile filling up in him, he did actually feel a short-lived pang in his stomach, he started

thinking about his wife, how she had been acting strangely, even more than was her habit, and

afterwards he felt a stinging pain spreading
through his abdomen followed by a kind of
heartburn, a flaming uneasiness scattering inside him, Bruce spoke again, Anderson didn't
listen to him, he heard him but he didn't listen.

"… and Dad picked up the phone he had
thrown against the wall. He put it down on the
table, grabbed the receiver and dialled a number. The phone rang a few times, Dad put down
the receiver, in truth he punched the table with
the receiver, our Alexei didn't say anything. He
wondered if Dad was mad because he had asked
about the KGB after the lady client's call. Our
Alexei had, I mean. As I told you before, dear
gentleman."

Anderson nodded, he looked at the tape recorder.

"Are you mad at me because I talked about
the KGB, Dad?", we asked, and Dad grunted
but did not reply.

Because it wouldn't be the first time Dad got
mad with our Alexei after he had asked about
the KGB, it's another secret issue, Dad seldom
talks about it, though he has never worked for

the KGB, according to him, he has only been recruited, or, in truth, the KGB agents tried to recruit him, and Dad never accepted. Besides, Dad couldn't and can't ever talk about the KGB anyway, as he was and is in an unknown location and we couldn't and can't talk to him, of course, for we didn't and still don't know where he was or is. Officially, at least", Bruce added after a short pause. "Officially, officially, I mean. Officially, Monsieur Detective", he concluded.

"Yes, yes, I got what you meant."

"I assumed you did, Monsieur Detective."

"Detective Anderson, please."

"Yes, Monsieur Detective Anderson, thank you."

"You're welcome. Well, I understood what you said, so you can proceed."

"And the people who are going to listen to the tape, Monsieur Detective Anderson?"

"What people? Who are you talking about?"

"The people who will make use of this recording. Prosecutors, judges, police. I think that's how you do it, right? They will use the recording if I'm not mistaken?"

"Yes, sure, you got it right."

"You see, that's what I'm talking about, Monsieur Detective Anderson."

"Yes… wait, what are you talking about?"

"About the people who're going to listen to this tape."

"Yes, yes, sure, but what about them?"

"They're the judges, the prosecutors…"

"Yes. I got it. I know who they are."

"But you just asked me about them."

"I did? Well yes, but not in that sense. Not *who* they are. And… Are you mocking me?"

"No, Monsieur Detective Anderson."

"Just Detective Anderson, please. No monsieur."

"Yes, Monsieur Detective Anderson. From now on I am going to call you only Detective Anderson, Monsieur Detective Anderson."

"God damn it, are you joking, or what?"

"I'm not, Detective Anderson. I swear."

"So what's the point of this conversation?"

"I don't know, Detective Anderson. You just asked about the people who'll listen to the tape."

"Yes, what about them?"

"They're the ones listening to the tape later. The judges, the prosecutors…"

"Oh, fuck me! I know who they are. I just asked why you mentioned them. What's the problem with the tape?"

"I was only wondering if they might not understand what I was saying."

"And what were you saying?"

"I said *officially*, and then repeated *officially*, as they may not understand what I had said."

"Don't worry, the tape recorder works fine, they will understand you. I can hear you quite perfectly, so will they, too."

"But you're listening to me face to face, Detective Anderson. They won't be."

"Yes, isn't that a shame?"

"I would say so, albeit one can't say that in this instance they're going to have as great a disadvantage as if I were a human person."

"You can bet they won't."

"Yes, Detective Anderson, I see you understood what I was hinting at. I don't have lips, and they won't be able to look at my lips while I speak. Or, let's say, on the other hand they won't miss looking at me while I do speak, insofar as regards to the fact they won't misinterpret me based on not looking at my moving lips while I speak, though they might, in fact, miss looking at me just out of curiosity. Do you think they may find it curious to look at me while I speak, Detective Anderson, dear gentleman?"

"Of course, I don't doubt they may… wait, god damn it, let's back to business."

"Yes, sorry, let's get back to the issue about Dad being officially in an unknown location. You see, they might not understand what I said, not only due to any recording problems, but also owing to a lack of comprehension of what I meant regarding Dad being *officially* in an unknown location. They wouldn't grasp the meaning…"

"They will! God, how they will grasp the meaning!"

Anderson rose from his chair, almost upturning it such was the fierceness of his movements. He grabbed his abdomen at once, feeling an intense pain in his bowels, like that of a screwdriver being twisted in his intestines. He hadn't ever felt a screwdriver being twisted in his intestines, but it seemed a good analogy, at least a few seconds later, not at the exact moment he felt the sting, or the first great sting, let's call it that way, for he felt a continuous stabbing in his middle-lower abdomen. Bruce continued talking, indifferent or apparently indifferent to Anderson's suffering. Bruce kept talking about the KGB, a KGB agent, then something about a CIA agent, or a Monsieur CIA Agent, who had reached out to Dad even before they fled from Pripyat back to Russia, Dad's Mother Russia, because Dad and Mom, god bless her and grant her eternal rest, as well as Babushka were all from Russia, to be more accurate from some Whatever-its-name oblast, Anderson couldn't really grasp it, the plush donkey once again mentioned the KGB, CIA and possible connections to the murder, and Anderson pondered if Bruce wasn't right after all, maybe there was some connection, perhaps Bruce or Alexei or someone from their family was working for one of those agencies, he and Mercier were possibly poisoned, truly poisoned, not by a semi-rotting hotdog eaten the day before and further decomposing in their innards, but by real poison, as poisoning foes was a long-time Russian tradition, the CIA preferred other methods, nevertheless one couldn't be sure. Anderson felt an atrocious stomach cramp and knelt on the floor.

Bruce was now only able to see his eyes, his forehead, and the top of his head.

"Detective Anderson, dear gentleman?"

Anderson groaned.

"I can't see you, Detective Anderson."

The detective groaned again.

"Detective Anderson, I feel this is quite rude on your part, I must say, dear gentleman."

Anderson cried and tried to get back on his feet. He couldn't manage to.

"Well, as you please. As I was stating, dear gentleman, Dad created me in that same workshop, or to be honest in another workshop, though quite similar to that one, and rather nearby, too, it used to be located a couple of streets away before it was demolished. Dad says they demolished it for political reasons."

Bruce didn't delve into the political question related to the demolishing of the previous workshop. Anderson didn't ask him either; he sighed and rolled a bit on the floor. Bruce stopped speaking for a moment. As Bruce was not at all a fan of Heidegger, he didn't believe in the possibility of accessing being by studying the human existence, which one may find reasonable enough a reason to ignore Heidegger's thinking, because one may argue that Heidegger was not a philosopher at all, but someone who obscured his language with the sole purpose of concealing his *lack of thought*, yes, Heidegger recurred to all the pretentiousness and pomp at his disposition to hide his *unphilosophical system*, as Bruce and many among the learned people think, but Bruce smiled to himself on establishing a parallel between a little pastiche of Heidegger's main concept and the empirical observation allowing him, Bruce, to assume that, from examining Detective Anderson's current existence, one could extract from his contortions how his being was under assault from toxic forces wreaking havoc on his innards, and to this may one defend Heidegger's moronic thinking by stating that Bruce was not establishing a parallel between Anderson's current gastrointestinal ordeals, but indeed applying solely a behaviouralist method or even a biology technique to probe Anderson's innards without directly analysing them. Notwithstanding Detective Anderson's internal turmoil, Bruce expected some poise from a law enforcement agent.

Detective Anderson? Well, I never… I find your behaviour somewhat unusual. I have never been in an interrogation room before, not even in a police station, but one can't but feel influenced by certain preconceived ideas taken from all kinds of cultural products. I would expect another posture from an agent of the law. Is that right, Detective Anderson? To call you an agent of the law?

Anderson seemed to have stopped moving altogether.

You know, dear gentleman, I was talking about Dad's old workshop, my birthplace, Bruce began, but I should also tell you about how Jean-Pierre disturbed Alexei on the day the woman was killed. I was on the windowsill when our Alexei arrived, we listened to Babushka's lamentations, she's not prone to wail, she hides her sufferings inside, our Alexei too, he can't be bothered to talk about his concerns, but I knew, yes, I saw it, or better yet, I heard his pain in his voice, his quavering. It's true he arrived to immediately open a letter sent to Babushka, a letter in which the dear gentlemen and ladies from the hospital called Babushka for an appointment with a medical doctor, and this scheduled meeting was to take place not many days after the letter's arrival. Please take into account that our Alexei found the letter on the exact day that 29 year-old woman, a blonde woman in her 30's, as some newspapers erroneously put it in the beginning and only later corrected, well, he found it on the day that woman was being killed before our Alexei fetched the letter left on the doormat, he entered our home, Babushka was sitting half lying on the couch, among pillows, this I know from her breathing, as you might remember, Monsieur Detective Anderson, sorry, Detective Anderson, your partner Monsieur Other Detective seems to be taking his sweet time wherever he went to, it's a mystery, what's he up to?, I wonder, but that's not really any of my business, I should stick to the matter at hand, I guess Dad programmed me too well, I absorbed too many of your human behaviours. How I wish I had been granted a more mathematical mind! Not that my core can't process complex equations and calculations, no, the problem lies in my propensity to jump from one line of thinking to another completely different line of thinking, albeit one may conclude this is not true, in fact they don't differ that much, these two hypothetical lines of thought, or in a certain sense they do, of course, it's just that they must possess a common thread, a little clog inserting itself in my mind's wheels, a shared fact, that's how the human brain functions, it's quite incredible if you take the time to ponder on it, it's amazing how the human brain can connect different dots in such a short time, in seconds, nanoseconds, you name it, my computer brain is even faster, though in the end I'm stuck with using human language in a way that can be understood by human brains other than mine, if you consider my artificial data processor a human brain, Dad programmed me well to accomplish that goal, Dad is in fact a genius, a genuine Russian spirit of knowledge, a heir of Russian and Soviet science, he beat them all, I'm his magnum opus, if only he could listen to me, he refuses to, the first time I spoke he threw me against a wall, just like he threw the phone against the wall that same day the woman was killed and Babushka got the letter from the hospital. Thus it may appear that it was a full day, a day rich in important or at least bizarre events, and you will ask yourself how that is possible, but please do pay attention, oh dear gentleman pray be careful when reaching conclusions, for thy conclusions might hold falsity and all that opposes fairness. So be kind enough as to follow me in my mental perambulations. You will therefore understand it was a normal day, that Dad's fury — common as it is — and receiving a letter — though from the hospital — are in themselves trivial occurrences, with the only incident worthy of note being the woman's murder. The two other incidents only seem relevant when linked to the murder, and this happens due to their chronological coexistence, not to some factual link, although it's not my responsibility to examine that. That's why I keep adding these details — so you, dear gentleman, and your colleague, another dear gentleman, can discern for yourselves what's worth what. And I don't get tired of talking, I need no water to moisten my lips, time is mine to replenish with words, as long as my batteries allow me to stay on.

Anderson didn't reply. Bruce thought it extremely rude, despite Anderson's possible intestinal suffering, and he vented his indignation.

In my opinion, if I'm allowed to have one, of course, since I'm not a citizen at all, this is preposterous and shameful, he said. You keep avoiding any eye contact with me. I'm worthy of your attention, dear gentleman. Of yours and your partner's, who's still missing. Where is he?

Anderson moaned, he was trying to get up.

Anyway, as you told me before, the tape recorder seems to be working fine, I'll just go through all these issues. I think it's important to have everything mentioned and done with, my too-human of a mechanical brain won't allow me to go ahead without talking about this problem with Jean-Pierre, and now I'm referring to Alexei's schoolmate Jean-Pierre, he's what one would call an upstart. A parvenu. Jean-Pierre thinks too much of himself, in my opinion, once I saw him, our Alexei took me with him to school, I spent all day inside his backpack. I could hear bits and pieces of conversation, first in the classroom, then outside, our Alexei didn't take me to the playground, then classes finished for the day and we walked home, we heard a high-pitched voice coming from behind us. We turned our head back and there he was, it was

Jean-Pierre, and two of his pals were not far away, they were quite close.

"Hey, Russky", he said to us.

We turned our heads, avoided looking at him.

"Where are you going?", he asked once we started walking away from him. "Don't you turn your back on me."

We kept walking home.

"Are you listening to me, Russky?"

We ignored him. Then he or one of his minions threw a handful of earth at us. We felt the impact on the backpack and turned round again.

"I'm not called Russky", we said.

"You're called what I want you to be called!", yelled Jean-Pierre.

"Is that so? Why?", we asked.

"Because you're poor and I'm not", he replied.

"You're stupid", we said.

"No, *you* are stupid."

"No, you're the one who's stupid."

"You're a thousand times stupider."

"You're infinite times stupider."

"You're… stupider… infinite times plus one stupider."

"That's just stupid."

"You're stupid, you moron!"

"Asshole!", we said, because Babushka couldn't hear us, she was at home, we were in the street, Jean-Pierre and his two minions approached us, the backpack was open, we saw them coming nearer, but they didn't do anything on that occasion, Jean-Pierre threatened us, he's an upstart alright, he has roots going all the way back to France, he told us another time, our Alexei and I were together, we weren't together on the day the woman was killed, or supposedly killed, but she died, no doubt about it, her death was already hanging in the air as a possible possibility of an occurrence, an eventual eventuality of fate, Monsieur Detective Anderson, sorry, perhaps you should check my batteries, I'm feeling itchy, you humans would call it itchy, if I'm not mistaken, or is it not itchy?, who can know, *how is it like to be a plush donkey with a capacity to reason and talk?*, now that's an interesting idea, a juicy philosophical question, let's study not only other species' points of view, but also other mechanical subjects, for I'm not a species, or I could be the first of a new species, a mechanical species, a hybrid between man, animal and machine, a mecha-donkey, we could write an interesting essay, I do have a lot of bibliography recorded in my mind, I do enjoy processing all those philosophy books, Alexei prefers comics and adventure books, we go to the library, we read comics and philosophy, I'm fonder of philosophy, we shall talk about that later, Detective Anderson. Anderson or Andersson, one or two S's? What did you say? Sorry, I can't hear you, detective. By the way, speaking of your name, are you a descendant of Nordic people? Anderson is quite a common name in Scandinavia, mostly in Sweden, but then it should be Andersson, with a double S, and as I haven't seen your name written down and can't hear what you say, I can't ascertain if you're Andersson or Anderson, though you could be a descendant of Nordic people even if your name's pronounced Anderson with a single S, not with a double S, and I'm assuming I got your name right, that you're called Anderson and not Andersen or Andresen, in which case you may also descend from Nordic people. You'd probably descend from Swedes if you're called Andersson, or let's say Anderson, as Anderson might also have been a corruption of your surname Andersson, dear gentleman, as was the case with many people arriving in the New World, namely in North America, maybe also in Central and South America, but surely in North America, but you'd most probably descend from Danes or Norwegians if you're called Andersen or Andresen. Then again you might descend from Brits, some Anderson coming from England, perhaps you descend from French people, from someone called Lebossu, or something like that, some criminal fleeing from Europe to the New World and changing his name upon arrival, you seem like the type of person to descend from a criminal, if you know what I mean, please don't be offended, Monsieur Detective Anderson, you seem to be doing some exercise down there, sadly I can't see, no doubt there's much to gain in observing your exercises, nevertheless it's quite true you seem to have that criminal facies so well described by scientists, and I've noticed you are afflicted with a lot of dandruff, perhaps it's not polite to refer this, but somehow I can't refrain from doing it, I'm feeling human, too human, there's an abundance of humanity filling me up to the brim, or let's say flowing out of my core, someone must tell you there's a big problem with you, there's dandruff everywhere, I wonder if there's a connection between the dandruff and your Nordic ancestry, I'm not hinting at a poor analogy, nothing on dandruff-snow, you have dandruff like snowflakes on your shoulders, not at all, no cheesy metaphors, dear gentleman, I wonder if it's some genetic problem, I have dealt mainly with Slavs, not Nordics, there's a lack of data hindering me from reaching conclusions regarding the prevalence of dandruff among specific groups of individuals as separated per genetic pattern... I have dealt with Slavs or genetically Slavic Canadians, almost all people I know belong to this particular group, except for Monsieur Pereira and his wife, besides, of course, such people as Mademoiselle Michelle the teacher and Jean-Pierre the young upstart, perhaps I can include the murdered woman in this list, as well as her murderer, the man who may be Portuguese, thus not a Slav. I will get back to that murderer's description, there are some details I can add, but let's wait for your partner, Monsieur Other Detective, if that's ok with you, Monsieur Detective Anderson, so I'm going to keep talking, you seem to be stretching or doing some other exercise, please don't bother listening to me, I'm a mere plush donkey, somehow I noticed our Alexei wasn't feeling well, that day Jean-Pierre had disturbed Alexei, I didn't know it when our Alexei arrived, but I found out later. The day before, Mademoiselle Michelle, Alexei's teacher, had both our Alexei and Jean-Pierre stay behind at the end of the day. She had found it strange that Alexei, our is Alexei such a good student, had had a terrible maths test, he had failed miserably, whilst Jean-Pierre, an incompetent student, had gotten his best mark ever, an almost perfect maths test. And she had made Jean-Pierre confess he had exchanged his test for Alexei's, he had erased Alexei's name and wrote down his own, then wrote Alexei's name on his test sheet, this he had confessed, and Alexei had felt flabbergasted. Mademoiselle Michelle had made Jean-Pierre apologize to Alexei, but he had called Alexei Russky in front of Mademoiselle Michelle, that was what had hurt him the most on Friday, as Mademoiselle Michelle has good titties and is very friendly and nice, we have noticed how she is nice and a beautiful woman, we would like to have a nice woman like Mademoiselle Michelle as our girlfriend one day, she's smart and kind, but Jean-Pierre is an asshole, Alexei was disturbed when he arrived home on Friday but not as much as he was on Saturday, the day of the murder, because he had met Jean-Pierre in the park, Jean-Pierre had scowled him and called him a snitch, so our Alexei came back home annoyed and picked up the letter to Babushka, I was on the windowsill and our Alexei only told me what had happened a couple of hours later, when the woman was arguably dead, and then I talked about her to Alexei and he told me we had to call the police, and we had to use a phone for the second time that day, as we had already used one in Dad's workshop, Dad had thrown it against the wall, his phone, of course, he had tried to do the same to me, but had done it only to his phone, he had picked it up from the floor, set it back on the workbench, it was not broken, and presently, at 11.11 a.m. he lifted the receiver and dialled a number, we waited while he called someone, he hung up at 11.15 a. m.

11.15 a.m.

This much is true: a couple of days after the murder Mercier and Anderson interrogated two suspects. First a man named Didier H., then a man named Michel L. No woman was interrogated, for the police thought it highly improbable that a woman might have committed the crime, not only due to the testimonies of two eyewitnesses — Monsieur Pereira and an old lady who lived in the victim's building — who claimed to have spotted a suspicious man leaving the premises, but also due to the wounds inflicted on the dead woman, as her mortal stab wounds seemed to have been made by a taller and stronger person. Forensics had concluded that she might have been killed by a person somewhat taller, but that the murderer was probably stronger than her, thus *possibly* a man, since she was a well-built woman. As the crime scene investigators concluded that the stab wounds had *possibly* been made by a man, Anderson and Mercier grabbed the first two men they could reasonably try to blame for the murder.

They both lived in the victim's building. The first one, Didier H., was a plumber and had a prior record of assault, a crime for which he had been sentenced to a few months of jail several years ago. Didier H. was plumbing away in the outskirts of Montreal at the time of the murder as determined by the coroner, and had been seen arriving home late that evening by that same old lady who had also seen a suspicious man leaving the building some hours earlier, and she had found that medium-height brown-haired man suspicious because he was medium-height, brown-haired and limped slightly. She might have not found him suspicious had he *only* limped when leaving the building, if he had limped but weren't medium-height and brown-haired, but as he had limped and was simultaneously medium-height and brown-haired, the old lady had found him shady, a quite different impression from the one she got when she saw Didier H. arriving at the building late that evening. The old lady, Madame Aubert, didn't find Didier H. questionable upon his arrival home from work. First and foremost because she didn't yet know her neighbour had been killed, so she wasn't particularly worried or alert to signs of criminal behaviour on the part of Didier H. or any of other of her neighbours (let us keep in mind that Madame Aubert had only found that stranger a queer-looking, doubtful character because he was medium-height, brown-haired and limping; she wasn't particularly intolerant herself — on most occasions); secondly, Didier H. usually got home from work late in the evening, often still wearing his plumber jumpsuit, except on Fridays, when he got home early and went out half an hour later to party and drink. So, that evening he had parked his plumbing van outside the building, opened the main door, taken the lift up to his flat's floor and, as far as Madame Aubert could determine, entered his flat to rest and spend the night. After hearing the lift cables screeching and its door opening, Madame Aubert had heard Didier H. belching (from drinking beer, she thought) and jingling his keys while opening his flat's door (Didier H. lived on the same floor as Madame Aubert). Madame Aubert had consequentially stopped thinking about Didier H., and instead had relaxed in her living room, where her tomcat Bébert had been resting for some hours, now waking up and scratching

Madame Aubert's ankle, a somewhat painful incident which engraved itself on the old lady's mind, and we might say this episode still stands out in her mind due to all the other incidents that happened that day, such as seeing the suspicious stranger leaving the building or knowing, later but not so later as to have yet forgotten what had happened on that evening, that one of her neighbours had been killed inside her flat, in the building they both *shared*, a fact even more conspicuous to her now ageing and enfeebled mind due to the so-called mental connections, because the murdered woman had once taken care of little Bébert for a few days while Madame Aubert was visiting her sister in Québec City. She had therefore an extremely good opinion of the dead woman, and this she told the police.

"I'm horrified. How could this have happened? And now, Detective, how's it going to be from now on?", she had asked one of the agents who had knocked at her door, and who happened to be Mercier.

"From now on? We are already investigating…", he said.

"No, no. Not that. About my Bébert."

"About your Bébert?"

"Yes. Do you think he'll be traumatized?"

"How so? Has he seen anything?"

"Oh, I guess so. He's not blind, Detective."

"Then can you call him here? We would like to talk to him", Anderson asked. He was standing beside Mercier.

"This is quite unexpected, Detective…", the old lady said, proceeding to call out for Bébert… Bébert, Bébert!... he who took his sweet time to show up at the door.

Both detectives looked down at the blackish-grey cat.

"But… It's a cat", Mercier said.

"Of course, Detective! I had a dog, too, my Snoopalloo, but he died so many years ago. And Bébert isn't getting any younger either."

"Yeah, but…", replied Mercier.

"Don't you believe me, Detectives? Just take a look at the poor thing! He's 17 years old. How long do you think he's going to live?"

"We don't know, M'am", they said.

"Look at him, at my dear Bébert! He's losing fur all the time."

And true enough, Madame Aubert petted Bébert and a big hairball came rolling over the floor and stopped at Anderson's feet.

"He's been losing so much fur, and the vet told us to use a paste, you know, a special pâté made for cats losing fur, so they can lick themselves and the fur sticks to the pâté in their stomach, and in the end they defecate the balls, or at least that's the idea, no one wants a furball stuck in their bowels, anyway it's been working fine so far. The problem is that I fear Bébert might lose even more fur now that he feels all these bad vibes. He knew the dead woman, you know. Poor thing."

"He knew her?", Anderson asked, his eyes on the cat.

"Sure, she took care of him once, when I went to visit my sister in Québec City", and Madame Aubert went on to tell them how everything had happened, including her satisfaction with the dead woman, to whom she had given a present last Christmas. Anderson and Mercier sighed, groaned, Mercier scratched his balls, he feared he had caught crabs, possibly from Anderson's wife. Madame Aubert picked up Bébert and almost shoved it into the detectives' faces, insisting that they take a look at the poor animal. "And he's neutered, see, you can even touch him and feel for yourselves. Please, don't be shy."

Mercier and then Anderson touched the cat's pudenda, or the place where his pudenda should have been. Nothing at all, and Mercier smiled a little while touching his balls and simultaneously Bébert's empty crotch. The cat began to purr, Mercier kept petting him. Anderson's interest was aroused and he too tried to pet Bébert. Both policemen were passing their hands over the cat's crotch when Madame Aubert resumed talking.

"You see, he's not feeling well", she said.

"He seems quite satisfied, if you ask me", Mercier replied. "He's even purring."

"But maybe he's sad, Detective! Who knows if he isn't?"

"I don't know", Mercier confessed.

"You don't? And you, Detective, do you know?", she asked while nodding to Anderson.

"Who, me? No, not at all", he replied.

"I thought so."

"Perhaps his vet knows?", Mercier suggested.

"His vet knows nothing. Once she couldn't
even tell me if he had parasites or gastritis. Can
you believe that? It's preposterous."

"Yes, indeed it is", the detectives agreed
while petting Bébert, who with his belly up was
purring in his owner's arms.

"And this vile crime… Poor Bébert, just imagine if he had heard something", Madame Aubert added.

"Yes, what if he had? What would have he
heard?", the two detectives asked.

"I don't know! I didn't hear anything. I only
saw that suspiciously shady man. And then,
well, yes I heard…"

"What?"

"The lift cables, the door. But only when my
neighbour came in in the evening."

"What neighbour?", the detectives asked,
and they understood they had finally found
their perfect suspect, at least for the day, as they
had no logical or illogical reasons to consider
him a suspect for several days. They might find
something to keep him on their radar for a few

more days, though they couldn't rationally expect to indeed find a clue or any hint of a trail allowing them to keep Didier H. in custody. Anyway, they were pleased to have found a perfect scapegoat for that day and possibly for that *night*, too. It meant Didier H. could spend the next 24 hours lingering in interrogation rooms, cells, unclean toilets and thug-packed corridors and halls. And — sheer perfection: he seemed the kind of man with sufficient physical endurance to sustain 24 hours of hunger, thirst, verbal abuse, and an occasional outburst of violence by another detainee. Yes, he was taller than Mercier and Anderson, who both went to fetch him at the house he was working in. Didier H. was plumbing up and down the house, whose deficient water system had plunged the house into a dark, damp hole… there was water everywhere… rivers of a brownish liquid running down the stairs… driftwood passing by… Anderson thought he had seen a beaver… a real beaver… like the ones he used to see when visiting his paternal grandparents in Ontario… it was a real beaver!... look there, Mercier, gosh, look!... what, you didn't see it?... oh, this fucker… nevertheless, Mercier found Didier

H., he was lurching behind a sink… so much water… Mercier was not fond of water, at least not of so much water… he had even rejected a trip to Venice… he was afraid of falling into the lagoon, into a canal… from a gondola... or even from a window… he even had a recurrent idea, he sometimes thought about writing a film script… or perhaps a television series script… submit it to a producer, maybe a Canadian producer, but he could also send it to a non-Canadian producer… a script about a flooded and abandoned Venice, where only a few remaining people inhabited the buildings' top floors… they went around in their boats, some died alone at home… it was nightmarish… an awful idea disturbing Mercier, he who looked at Didier H. hunched over a pipe. Water was flowing out of that pipe, Mercier called out to Didier H., Anderson called out to him, too. Didier H., still hunched over the damaged pipe, grunted some unintelligible words, grabbed a wrench, pounded it on the sink, the noise echoed throughout the house, water kept flowing down the stairs, Anderson saw another beaver, though it was probably the same beaver he had seen before, he pointed it out to Mercier, his partner was then asking Didier H. to please accompany them to the police station, they had some business to take care of. Didier H. told them he too had business to take care of, meaning that punctured pipe which was causing so much disaster all over that house, and even threatening to flood the entire street. Mercier stood his ground, he grabbed on to the lavatory for further support, avoiding being taken by the strong current, god damn it, turn off the water, exclaimed Anderson, he too reaching for a piece of driftwood… almost fighting over it with a beaver… now he had no doubts, it was a real beaver… then he grabbed the doorframe, tried to remain in the corridor, his trousers were completely wet… up to his crotch… Mercier was still holding firm to the lavatory… Didier H. finally managed to turn off the water… he had crossed the bathroom to the walled-in faucet next to the lavatory… the pipe stopped pumping water into the bathroom and a beaver immediately swam towards the bathtub.

"I told you!", Anderson yelled at the door. "Didn't I tell you?", he asked Mercier.

"Yes, yes, you told me", Mercier replied.

"Yes… but what did I tell you?", Anderson asked while the remaining water flowed out of the bathroom.

"What are you talking about?"

"What did I tell you, exactly?"

Anderson and Mercier continued exchanging questions and answers, most of them starting with *what*, and Didier H. soon began wondering *why* — why was he a plumber?, why was he wet up to his crotch when he had been called to solve a simple problem (the house's owner had told him it was just a leaky faucet)?

"And there's more than one!", Anderson yelled.

Truth be told, four beavers were now visible in the faint light coming from the corridor, the bathroom light was still turned off, that is the truth, they had not only faced a gang of working beavers and a flood, but they also faced a gang of working beavers and a flood *in semi-darkness* and thus in *utterly uncomfortable circumstances*, but before Anderson and Mercier could ponder on how four beavers had reached the second floor of a house on the outskirts of Montreal, Didier H. was sitting in a interrogation room, which, contrary to the incidents in the bathroom, might indeed turn both detectives towards the right path and therefore allow them to find the murderer. One might feel there's no sufficient pathos in this scene, that there isn't *enough seriousness* in this narrative, it can't be a weighty description of a crime if in the inter-mezzos one finds episodes which include beavers in flooded bathrooms or, to be more precise, beavers in a dark, damp bathroom where the dripping pipe causing the water leak and flooding the entire house is located. According to Alexei, our Alexei, those beavers could arguably be called *phenomena*. "If you don't know what something is or why it happens, then it's called a *phenomenon*", he would say, and Bruce the stuffed donkey would nod, if he could nod, but he would agree with him for sure. "And the correct plural of phenomenon is phenomena", Alexei would add; Bruce would once again agree.

"I'm fed up with this. We're going nowhere with these shenanigans", Major Rawls said as soon as he rushed through the door and into the interrogation room.

"But…", Anderson and Mercier replied.

"I don't want to hear any more excuses! So far, you still got nothing", he yelled. Then he noticed Didier H. sitting at the table. "Who's this bum?"

"He's a suspect", the detectives said.

"Is he?"

Major Rawls looked at Didier H. like he couldn't believe that man was a possible murderer, although Didier H. was indeed tall and strong, butter wouldn't melt in his mouth, or so it seemed. Anyway, Major Rawls would have known Anderson and Mercier had nothing on Didier H., his being a neighbour of the victim with only a criminal record and having arrived home late in the evening of the murder not being enough to detain him, though Rawls would certainly approve of his detectives' methods, if only for the temporary respite they granted him and the department, the media and his superiors pressing him for answers, the murder was still fresh, but people demanded answers as soon as possible. It wasn't possible, as it was years ago, to supress this demand for answers, not at all, people wanted to know *who* killed *who,* and *when* and mostly *why* they were killed, yes, that was the main goal of the media

and the news bulletins as demanded by readers
and listeners and watchers, all of them eager to
know who killed that 29-year-old blonde
woman, above all why she had been killed,
there must have been one or several reasons for
the crime to have been committed, perhaps she
was a drug addict and owed money to her
dealer, she was peradventure dating a married
man and his wife had killed her or hired someone to kill her, although it would certainly be
possible that her lover had murdered her because she was pregnant and he didn't want to
have any children, or he might want to have
children, but not with her, as she was crazy and
boring and addicted to drugs perchance he
would have even wanted to have children with
her, he just couldn't allow her to give birth to a
child because he was married to a rich woman
whom he preyed upon as a good predator-para-
site and who would have divorced him had she
known he was having an affair and was about to
have a baby with another woman, either because she couldn't herself get pregnant or
plainly because she had already had children
with him and was jealous of the other woman

and her child-to-be. Maybe both of them, husband and wife, had planned to kill the blonde 29-year-old woman after the husband had confessed he was having an affair, he thus being the murderer or both of them hiring a hitman to do the job, and let's not forget the murderer, as described by Bruce, was supposedly a medium-height brown-haired man who could definitely be a Portuguese man or someone corresponding to the commonest Portuguese phenotype, so at least one knew the victim hadn't been killed by a woman, the forensics had excluded this hypothesis, albeit not with full certainty and still unofficially by that time, anyway, despite all the time allocated to that mission they couldn't actually obtain scientific proof that the murder hadn't been perpetrated by a woman, a tall and strong woman, it was a possible if improbable hypothesis, after all, men are generally not only taller but also violent gorillas, and Bruce's testimony pointed directly at a man as the culprit, though at the time of Didier H.'s interrogation that same fact wasn't yet known, better still, it was known to some, as Bruce and Alexei and Andrei had indeed called the police, but it was not *taken into account*, instead disregarded as false information, a prank from the brothers Andrei and Alexei, or at least a fantasy of Alexei, because Alexei had indeed told his brother Andrei there was a dead woman or a presumably dead woman lying on the floor in a flat in the opposite building, then proceeded to call the police, and he had added that Bruce had seen a man leaving the dead woman's flat, first to Andrei, afterwards to the police, via Andrei, tell them Bruce saw a man, Andrei told them, and Andrei had done so, though omitting the witness's name, Bruce, but as Alexei listened to the call he yelled that it had been Bruce who had seen a medium-height brown-haired man leaving the dead woman's flat, and the agent on the line asked who Bruce was, to which Alexei at once replied Bruce was his plush donkey, Bruce is my plush donkey, he yelled at the receiver Andrei was still holding.

"Your donkey?"

"Yes, my plush donkey", Alexei yelled, now grabbing the receiver.

"Is it a plush donkey?"

"Who?"

"Who?"

"Who?"

"What?"

"What what?"

"Who's the guy you were talking about?"

"What guy?"

"The one your brother was talking about. Is he your brother? He is, right?"

"Who? Bruce? No, he isn't."

"He isn't? So is he your father?"

"Bruce? No!"

"So who is he?"

"My plush donkey."

"Your plush donkey?"

"Yes. Mine."

"But I spoke with him just a moment ago."

"With Bruce? Impossible, he's on the windowsill."

"How old are you, lad?"

The police had registered all the information, despite disregarding the details on the so-called murderer as pure invention from Alexei (*aged 10, boy in the front building, called together with his brother*). Nonetheless, they had considered the remaining info veritable enough to send two patrol cars to the supposed victim's building. The patrol cars' sirens alerted all the neighbourhood and therefore the local press, which afterwards stirred the national media's attention. News of the murder was then released throughout the country, leading to the usual pressure on the police, and Major Rawls was feeling a bit too displeased, for he wanted to play some golf, leave Montreal and spend a few days away from his wife only playing golf, yes, therefore, because he was too displeased and under pressure to focus, he had not read the reports as indeed he should have, thus not knowing, as he should have but he didn't, that there was no rational reason to interrogate or, moreover, detain Didier H., and that his detectives could at the most ask Didier H. some questions regarding his neighbour the murder victim, inquire if he had seen or knew something relevant to the investigation, a minor incident, had he heard a cry for help, did he known the victim?, for how long?, did Didier H. feel any attraction to her, did she reject his physical and sexual advances on her?, Didier H. could have tried to seduce her and not accepted her rejection, then tried to kill her or hire someone to do it. Rawls would have known, had he read Mercier's and Anderson's report, that this was most surely pure bullshit, but for the time being it was good enough, and Rawls wouldn't yet read any report, only pretend to, as he needed only a respite to breathe a little and play some golf, so he took a look at Didier H., then turned his back on him, waved to call Anderson and Mercier to the door.

"Put some pressure on the motherfucker. He doesn't look innocent to me", he whispered to them, but somehow Didier H. did overhear the word *motherfucker*, and straightened himself in his chair.

Both detectives nodded, Rawls strode along the corridor whistling a song back to his office, Anderson closed the door, Mercier turned the tape recorder on, Anderson cleared his throat and sat facing Didier H.

"So, now we are recording our conversation. Do you understand that?", he asked Didier H.

"Yes", Didier H. replied.

"Do you understand all your answers are being recorded and can be used in a court of law?", Anderson insisted.

"Yes, I do."

"Please do tell us your full name, age, address and occupation."

Didier H. told them his full name, age, address, and occupation. Anderson and Mercier then briefly told Didier H. he could have a lawyer with him at the interrogation, but they didn't delve much in that, as they wanted *only to ask him a few questions*, so they wouldn't unnecessarily waste his time. Didier H. was still thinking about the rotting pipe, he had left it mid-job and he feared the water had begun flowing out again, flooding the second storey, the first storey, the ground floor, reaching the street... attracting the beavers... by that time they had probably already built a damn in the stairway... but Didier H. also had his mind full of his own personal dreams and wishes and lustful desires mingling into a plumber's gluing paste of confused thoughts, Didier H. had his head not only *devastated* by plumbing issues, so well-known to him, but also *havocked* by for-him-quite-surprising academic pretentions, he had abandoned school as early as possible, however he now intended to study at university, for he believed he could bang that art student he had met half a year before, the one with cute black-rimmed glasses and long hair, a frail pallid-skinned girl younger than him, he still had hopes to make sweet love to her, despite her quite obvious rejection of his advances. I don't want to see you again, she had said once, and she had repeated it on the next occasions, I told you I didn't want to see you, didn't I?, she had said over and over again, and truth be told, Didier H. did think of kidnapping her or even murdering her, he was a beast and a possible murderer at heart, yes, a plumber with a desire to study art, not only because he wanted to bang that art student, but also because he so wished to study English and perhaps some French, he was genetically half French, half English, so one can say he had a *genetic interest* in the arts, he had a so-called *genuine personal interest* in the art student he so much wanted to bang, and a genetic interest in the arts, so he had a *double interest* in the arts, which is no doubt natural, as possibly everyone has a double, triple or even *quadruple* interest in a matter one desires to further study, some want to study a certain subject for their personal pleasure and to earn money, others just to earn money and therefore get all kinds of perks and acknowledgement in their profession, so, it's always at least a double interest, and often a triple interest, as they may want to study that matter by choice, to earn money and to please their family, for example, now that's a triple interest in something, so Didier H. had a double interest in the arts, which was natural, but he had also bad instincts towards women, namely that pallid-skinned student. As Didier H. was indeed a scumbag, he might have redirected his lustful criminal urges toward his neighbour. He had not, though. Didier H. was innocent of that murder and would remain innocent of any murder for 31 more years. Anyway, he himself didn't know that yet. He kept pondering on his life and life in general. What am I doing here?, he thought to himself, I should be fixing that pipe, he was afraid the house's owner would get there before him and come upon the beavers' damn or a rotting-wooden staircase… she would demand a repa-ration… he would have to reimburse her and even pay an extra sum for the carpentry repair work… he was friends with a carpenter, a true jack-of-all-trades, not a real certified carpenter but still good enough for the job, he could strike a deal with his friend and save some money… nevertheless he wouldn't make any profit from the job and would even lose money, both on the wood repair work and by having lost any other possible jobs he might had accepted… no beers that week… no hockey game either… he needed to get on the job as soon as possible, he wanted to get that through with, the interrogation, of course, in order to rest his weary and distressed mind, I want to get this over with, he thought, tonight he'd go to bed early, these guys are disgusting one is covered in dandruff what a mess he must have noticed how much dandruff he has on his shoulders, Didier H. thought, the other guy was repellent too, gosh the guy is taking one finger to his nose his nostril stretching it and the guy has the nerve to look at me at the same time oh no now he's rolling the booger, Didier H. was not only watching this grotesque scene, but also mentally describing it for our benefit, we the readers, I the narrator, you the reader, us both the readers of his mental incursions, now how would we know Mercier was rolling a booger he had pulled out from his nostril (which one?) if Didier H. hadn't taken the trouble to describing this horrid situation, he could have watched it, assimilated it through his brain and then kept it to himself or later tell it to a friend, maybe that carpenter friend of his,

perchance to a lady friend, she would find it preposterous, Didier H. found it preposterous too,
he could have *only watched and assimilated*
that situation, nonetheless he, confused as he
was, *felt the urge to tell us*, through his mental
digressions, what he was watching whilst sitting
face to face with Anderson, Mercier searching
deeply in his nose right behind Anderson, the
latter touching a piece of paper with his pen,
then pointing to the tape recorder on the table
between him and Didier H.

"Did you know Mademoiselle Forrestier?",
Anderson asked.

"Yes, I did. Well, barely."

"How barely? Can you explain your acquaintance with her?"

"I didn't know her that much."

"Did you know her name before?"

"Yes, I knew her name was Forrestier",
Didier H.

"You knew it? How did you know it?"

"Because she told me her name was Forrestier."

"She told you that? When did she tell you
her name was Forrestier?"

"Once… a few years ago, when she moved into our building."

"Can you be more precise in regard to the date?"

"I can't remember the date. It was a few years ago. Three years ago?"

"Don't ask me, I wasn't there."

"No, you weren't."

"Are you sure?"

"Of…?"

"That I wasn't there."

"There when I met her?"

"Yes."

"You weren't."

"So, I wasn't there when you met Mademoiselle Forrestier. When did that happen?"

"I told you I don't know. Some three years ago, maybe. I don't know."

"It must have been when she moved into your building, right?"

"Sure."

"Then when did she move into your building?"

"I don't know."

"Who knows, then?"

"When she moved into that flat? I don't."

"You don't, but who does know?"

"I don't… well, maybe her landlord."

"Do you know if she had a landlord? Or a landlady?"

"No, I don't. But maybe she did have one."

"Maybe she did, maybe she didn't", Anderson said. Mercier was still picking his nostrils, Didier H. was sweaty, his hands sticky.

"Yes, you can investigate that, right?", Didier H. suggested. Mercier stopped digging in his nose, Anderson shook all over, widening open his eyes. They both looked at him in silence. Then Anderson resumed speaking.

"Are you saying we don't know how to do our work?"

"No, not at all."

"So what are you saying?"

"Nothing."

"You are refusing to cooperate, I take it?"

"No, not at all!"

"You seem to repeat yourself a lot… And you aren't cooperating."

"How so?"

"When did you meet Mademoiselle Forrestier?"

"For the first time?"

"Yes."

"I don't know… As I told you, some three years ago. She was moving into our building, I met her in the lift."

"And that's when she told you who she was and her name?"

"No, not then."

"No? But you told me you learned her name when you met her for the first time?"

"Did I?"

"Yes."

"Are you sure I told you it was on the first time I met her?"

"Yes, I am."

"When I met her for the first time? Not just when she was moving?"

"No, no, when you met her for the first time. It's all recorded here", Anderson said, and he tapped gently the recorder. "Are you insinuating that I'm lying?"

"No, not at all."

"Now there you have it! Once again repeating your own words! *No, not at all!*"

"Yes… but isn't that allowed? After all, I'm just talking…"

"Just talking indeed. And perhaps lying."

At this moment, Didier H. thought about asking for a lawyer. But as he kept silent, Anderson soon got back to his query.

"You told us you found out your late neighbour's name when you first met her. Or when she was moving into your building. We don't know for sure when. You can't tell us. Three years ago, maybe. So, this is what we know", Anderson said. Then he paused for a second. "What we don't know, which is quite a lot, is, only to give you a simple example, how you actually got to know her name. How did you get to know her name, exactly?"

"I asked her what her name was."

"You did? When?"

"I told you before: some three years ago."

"Yeah… but on which specific occasion?"

"Well, I met her at the main door of the building."

"And then you asked her her name."

"Yes."

"But why then? Why not before? When you first met her."

"When I first met her?"

"Yes. In the lift, right?"

"Yes, in the lift."

"Why didn't you ask her then?"

"Because she might have been a visitor, or something."

"So you thought she might have been a visitor when you first met her in the lift?"

"No. Or something, maybe. I think I didn't think anything in particular about her."

"You didn't think anything….", Anderson said, and he scribbled on his piece of paper… dandruff fell from his head… from his shoulders. "Yet you remember seeing her in that lift, even now that three years have passed."

Didier H. didn't reply, as he didn't know if he was supposed to say anything.

"Don't you find it quite strange?", Anderson added.

"What?"

"That you didn't talk to Mademoiselle Forrestier when you first met her, and that you even thought her to be a visitor or didn't even thought about her. Yet despite not thinking about her, you do still remember her three years after that first encounter in the lift."

"Well… I… no, I don't think it's strange."

"How so?"

"I… must have remembered her because a couple of days later I talked to her."

"On that second meeting. It was the second time you saw her, right?"

"Yes."

"So why did you talk to her on that second occasion?"

"I…"

"And I find this quite odd: how come you don't know her first name?"

"Excuse me?"

"Do you know her first name?"

"No, I…"

"Because you never told us you know it. Do you?"

"No, I don't."

"So you didn't ask her?"

"I didn't, I just introduced myself."

"And how did you do that? Did you tell her your surname only?"

"I said something like 'Hello, I'm H…'"

"Oh, yes, that's nice, isn't it, Mercier?"

"It sure is", agreed Mercier.

"But do you believe it, Mercier?", Anderson asked, once again without looking at his partner, his eyes glued to Didier H.

"No, I don't."

"Of course you don't. You wouldn't present yourself to a young woman, your new neighbour, with just Mercier!", Anderson said, and he banged his fist on the table. "You would say 'Hello, I'm Jean Mercier, your neighbour. How do you do?' Wouldn't you, Mercier?"

"Yes, I would. That's what I would say", agreed Mercier, now supporting himself on Anderson's chair.

"You see, Mercier isn't exactly a charming person or a seducer, yet he would present himself as Jean Mercier, and not just Mercier, should he meet a neighbour for the first time. Or second time. Well, at least on the first occasion he'd talk to her", Anderson said. Mercier closed his fists, he clenched his teeth and got red in the face. So I'm not a seducer, he thought, oh, if you only knew!, he thought to himself, he didn't say a single word, not aloud, he talked to himself, oh this cuck I'm not a charming person you piece of shit you're going to see it, and so on and so forth went his thoughts. "It doesn't make any sense", Anderson added.

"It doesn't?", Didier H. asked.

"No."

"But why?"

"It's contrary to logic."

"How so?"

Anderson didn't reply at once, because he mostly enjoyed pondering on logical relations and syllogisms. He was indeed an amateur philosopher, or at least an amateur student of philosophy, as he had yet to compose any piece of work or create any kind of philosophical system. Nonetheless, he had recently read Wittgenstein's *Tractatus Logico-Philosophicus*. Actually, it had took him months to read it, and he therefore not only read it, but also *absorbed* it. In a sense, Anderson had imbibed the *Tractatus*, he had read it thoroughly and assimilated it as much he could assimilate any work. He had spent hours and hours and days and days reading it, he was reading it while Mercier was having an affair with his wife (Anderson's wife, of course), he had read it to the point of dreaming about it, he dreamt of *Tractatus*, some nights he even dreamt of Wittgenstein himself, Wittgenstein was building a house for his sister, because Wittgenstein had built a house for his sister with *his own hands*, that was the most relevant detail of Wittgenstein's biography and of the dream he had had of Wittgenstein, and Wittgenstein could have hired a contractor to build a house for his sister, or even buy an already built house for his sister, but he decided on building a house for his sister with his own hands, and that in itself could be more important than even his *Tractatus*, at least that was a valid conclusion if one would listen to a guy Anderson had met in a lecture on Wittgenstein, for Anderson had not only read Wittgenstein's *Tractatus*, he had also attended a free lecture at the university, a session on Wittgenstein given by a Professor. Anderson had met one attendee when he had gone to the toilet during a ten-minute break, he met that attendee in the men's toilet, the man in question, a stranger to him, was laughing in front of the mirrors, those mirrors hanging above the sinks, he was laughing and rubbing his hands, he often pressed the faucet rod to get water running, he would scrub his hands under water and then the faucet would turn off and he at once would rub his hands together, he talked aloud, apparently to himself but not really, he was a middle-aged grey-haired man, neither tall nor short, he was mocking another conference attendee, the one who, a few minutes before the break, had interrupted the Professor who was instructing the audience on Wittgenstein, that attendee had raised his arms in the air and waved, the Professor had stopped talking, yes, sir, any questions, he thought the attendee would ask him something about Wittgenstein's philosophical system, the audience though not vast showed itself eager to listen all ears pricked up for the question to come what question is it we want to know oh lord this guy was paying attention we weren't a shame a shame a shame most of us were sleeping the Professor's voice had put us under a monotonic spell it was a post-lunch lecture the majority of us the attendees were indeed middle-aged or old-aged none of us actually young all of us had difficult or at least slow digestion we could eat a medium-heavy lunch and ruminate on it for hours on end stomachal juices flowing up our oesophagi blurts of air coming out our mouths nostrils eyelids closing little by little millimetre by millimetre the Professor talking then suddenly one of us is waving his arms up in the air look come on look we elbow each other wake up man look here comes a question anyhow there'll be one of us asking the lecturer at least one question perhaps we could avoid altogether asking some final questions unnerving minutes with no end suspended cliff-hanger on unspoken words waiting for someone to speak up and vent their interrogations and doubts and opinions while the lecturer looks at us and searches for a victim dear gentlemen dear ladies pray do tell us what you think about the matter at hand so now here we had one of us parleying he was a middle-aged man just like that attendee Detective Anderson would later but not much later find in the toilet Anderson himself wasn't exactly middle-aged yet or maybe he was a mature man of 46 he could definitely be regarded as a middle-aged man in many societies including ours or let's say the Western contemporary society longevity is increasing middle-age hence increasing in its range or on the contrary shortening now right now possibly shortening after reaching its peak let's assume nowadays a Canadian needs to be 55 or over to be considered middle-aged probably closer to 60 as it seems but since this is happening in the 1990's and despite all the awful effects of civilization on current human longevity let's give it a break and say he was middle-aged already as life expectancy was actually a bit lower despite the aforementioned effects the now as we speak longer effects of chemicals and stress on people's health water pollution destroying corroding from inside running in our veins longevity will thus stop increasing altogether younger people dying of cancerous stress related diseases shortening their lives diminishing their quality of life capitalism burning grassland pastures invading forested areas cows and cows and cows poultry each human eating pounds and pounds of meat suffering destruction deforestation Americans eating more than any other people on earth drilling the planet for oil wars the CIA they even tried to recruit Alexei's dad now a Canadian post-Soviet citizen all mankind consumes too much though some countries less than others Americans still the kings of waste meat fish oil exploration conflicts poverty environmental disaster worse than them are only the Portuguese they barely frack yet they eat the most codfish in the world it's a codfish genocide Portuguese have been committing a codfish genocide for centuries sure not as intensive in their fishing as the new American Chinese Russian British Australian enormous ships whole towns on board of a ship except

there's only a few seamen there are many more
Americans than Portuguese it's true more Canadians than Portuguese albeit fewer Canadians
than Americans but the Portuguese have ex-
isted for a longer time nine centuries eating fish
not burning so much oil not so much meat either
but still nine centuries of consuming and cut-
ting trees no other people fells and maim-clips
trees with so much enthusiasm and out of such
a complete lack of necessity as the Portuguese
others might fell trees for profit lumbering away
rain forests ancient forests selling valued timber
Portuguese fell trees for pleasure or out of displeasure with life in no other country are trees
so abused cities and towns and villages streets
devoid of shade the natural shade of trees and
also the artificial shade it's another genocide
ecocide treecide arboretumcide their summers
so hot their sun so aggressive one may fall ill or
die of sun exposure heat waves wildfires still
they fell trees they hate nature and green and
trees everything green Portuguese love concrete cement grey surfaces the sun shining on
them flushing the Portuguese already feeble-
minded and short-constituted and monkey-like
at the most medium-height as per told by Bruce

describing the possible 29-year-old woman's killer a simian creature no doubt he too could fell trees kill women and cut down trees what a disgusting beast Portuguese fell trees to get more sun exposure this we have seen with our own eyes as if they didn't have enough sun already more precious sunrays for their mediocre indigestible cabbages and mostly to dry their miserable out-of-fashion clothes they hang them on clotheslines and in indoor moist laundry rooms in summer temperatures reach up to 40 degrees Celsius in some areas often up to more than 40 degrees Celsius in some areas and please do take into account we're talking about Celsius degrees not using the Fahrenheit scale it becomes scorching hot in the land of the Portuguese who cut down forests trees gardens parks mostly to get more sun exposure and some timber for toilet paper it's one of the biggest industries in Portugal back in the 90's it was already one of the biggest industries in Portugal they could we mean the Portuguese in general or their government let's say in general as in the Portuguese people well they could use wood in other industries other than the paper industry and especially in the toilet paper industry at that time they even barely used recycled paper in the production of toilet paper they in fact felled trees eucalyptus trees the whole country is full of them imagine that an invasive species from Australia moreover they cut down the indigenous forests and exchange them for eucalyptus plantations an ugly Australian species prone to wildfires Portuguese do actively destroy their own land they descend from other humanoids the children of intercourses of Neanderthals with monkeys the last Neanderthals lived in what is today and has been for centuries Portugal enclosed by its borders the oldest in Europe and possibly in the whole world almost nine centuries confining within its borders people who despise nature and trees people who often spilled like a poisonous liquid from their country's brim and smudged other countries and continents they have even built a transcontinental empire the Portuguese Empire long-lived and older than the British Empire but less famous Portuguese never had any talent for marketing can sell neither their products nor their image barely their language and then only due to Brazil they just can't sell anything or anyone if Bruce were a Portuguese author as he

intends to write novels one day he could be a
Portuguese writer but he's not Portuguese were
Bruce Portuguese he could have even killed
that 29-year-old woman Mademoiselle Forrestier to get some attention that's how they
promote themselves in Portugal where they kill
the indigenous forest to plant eucalyptus and
produce toilet paper meanwhile destroying everything sweltering everything the air contaminated with carbon monoxide the soil scorched
poisoned and all this in exchange for rolls of toilet paper not even to sell timber to produce
chairs like the ones we the lecture attendees
were sitting in made of good Canadian wood we
cherish our forests and trees and lumber here in
Canada only our digestion isn't so good anymore now we the lecture attendees have
reached middle-age but detective Anderson is
still not too old he somehow manages to digest
his lunch though he must empty his bladder
like all humans and animals at least we think all
animals must do it then he met a guy at the toilet he was mocking the attendee who had interrupted the lecture we woke up we had been
dozing off so this guy was paying attention let's
hear what he has to say, and he spoke out loud.

"You know, Wittgenstein built a house for his sister. With his own hands."

Surprised as we were, we didn't say a word, not one of us spoke, not even Anderson or the Professor. Then at last one of us, the attendee whom Detective Anderson would later meet in the toilet, spoke up: "What so? I built a house myself."

He had built a house with his own hands too… although not for his sister … because he didn't have one… if had one, he surely could have built her a house… with his own bare hands… no gloves!... with no heavy machinery at his disposal… if he only had a sister… or even a daughter… The Professor listened to his little story, and the first attendee interrupted the second attendee.

"He built it with his own hands", he said. "With his own hands", he repeated, glancing at the lecturer.

"But with his bare hands? No gloves?", the second attendee asked.

Then the first attendee turned around to look at him, as he was sitting in the first row of seats, he was sitting up front near the lecturer, while the second attendee was sitting a couple of rows behind him, he turned around to look at him, he said "It's quite impressive, if one thinks about it. He built a house with his own hands."

"Yes, that's quite impressive", the second attendee agreed. "But, listen, I too built a house with my hands. And with only a concrete mixer! And a bucket. With a hole in it!", he added, turning back to face us. "So, what's so special in that?", he asked, and a few of us smiled or laughed, the rest of us kept silent, "And surely he only designed it! I can't believe this fancy-pants Wittgenstein could build a house with his own hands!", he proclaimed, "I just can't believe it. It takes some hard, rough hands to build a house, I tell you!"

The so-called second attendee was hysterical... mortified... he couldn't be calmed down... we strained to ease his affliction, but failed... the so-called first attendee insisted on Wittgenstein having built his sister a house with his *own hands,* bare or not, as he couldn't ascertain if he had used work gloves... but with no assistance, there was no doubt about it... only he and himself working on it... the Professor tried to get the lecture back on track, nevertheless he had lost his train of thought, we listeners were restless, we couldn't focus on his words. The Professor told us we would have a 10-minute break, he looked at his watch and announced a 10-minute break. We the listeners then proceeded to walk down the hall and to the small bar, some of us went to the toilets, both the men's and ladies' toilets, where —in the men's toilet in particular — Detective Anderson met the so-called second attendee, who had built a house with his own hands (and a bucket with a hole and a concrete mixer), though sadly not for his sister, as he hadn't one, probably he had asked his parents for a sibling, either a brother or a sister, nonetheless they hadn't complied with his wishes, he had no siblings, or at least no sisters. Even though Anderson didn't inquire about his siblings, he knew the so-called second attendee had no sisters whatsoever, maybe he had had a sister previously, and then lost her, or perhaps he had never had a sister to begin with. He could still have one or several brothers, albeit Anderson would bet he hadn't any by the way he talked, call it some kind of gut feeling, so appropriate in that men's toilet, even though he could surely conclude, if he so wished, that the so-called second attendee, who with open arms he found mocking the so-called first attendee, *had in fact* at least one sister, as precluded by Wittgenstein's philosophical system, for Detective Anderson had indeed read his *Tractatus* and taken notes during the lecture. Hence, he knew that, according to Wittgenstein, the world is, quoting, the totality of *facts, not of things,* and that the world being the case and determined by the facts, still quoting, and by these being all the facts, because the totality of facts determines both what is the case, and (quoting!) also that is not the case, thus *the facts in logical space are the world.* Moreover, and I am quoting Herr Wittgenstein here, and please do pay attention, *in logic nothing is accidental: if a thing can occur in an atomic fact the possibility of that atomic fact must already be prejudged in the thing,* and (quoting, quoting, quoting) that *it would, so to speak, appear as an accident, when to a thing that could exist alone on its own account, subsequently a state of affairs could be made to fit.* So, in short, *if things can occur in atomic facts, this possibility must already lie in them.* And, quoting yet: *A logical entity cannot be merely possible. Logic treats of every possibility, and all possibilities are its facts.* And so on and so forth, propositions upon propositions burning themselves into Detective Anderson's brain, he studied them thoroughly, took notes, filled whole notebooks with his scribbling, logic, possibilities, facts, Wittgenstein's house, no, that was not important, he refused to inquire further on that topic, he wouldn't delve into that matter, he was more concerned with the philosophical consequences of Wittgenstein's logic on his life. Maybe not on his life, rather on his work, although one could state or at least assume and not state it, henceforth think concludingly assuming and yet not affirming that Detective Anderson's life was, then, in great part limited to his professional tasks, his job being his sole reason to live. At home he read the *Tractatus* and other books on the *Tractatus*, when home he read Wittgenstein's major work and other outputs of Wittgenstein, he read them both at home and out. Whenever he told his wife he was doing an extra shift staying until late in the evening at the police station he was in truth in a cafeteria somewhere in Montreal reading Wittgenstein's books and articles. At home he didn't have to lie, for his wife could see how he kept reading the *Tractatus* and other works of Wittgenstein in their living room and often in their bedroom. She could see him reading and studying Wittgenstein's works, the *Tractatus* but not only the *Tractatus*, every time she was home, which seldom happened anymore. She would frequently find Anderson reading Wittgenstein's works or works on Wittgenstein's works, but she seldom found him at home, as she rarely was home herself. Indeed she knew quite for sure that her husband lied when he told her he was working late — when he was in fact reading Wittgenstein —, because she was having an affair with Mercier, his work colleague and long-time partner, so she knew he wasn't working on a case, for she was actually banging Mercier while Anderson was supposedly working late in the evening, and Anderson couldn't be working late in the evening if she was banging Mercier *at the exact moment* Anderson was allegedly working on a case, inasmuch as Mercier and Anderson worked together as partners, which made it highly improbable for Anderson to be working late in the evening, since Mercier would at least be informed about that precise situation and know if he was working, and probably he too would have to work late in the evening, being his partner as he was. In short, Madame Anderson knew her husband wasn't working late in the evening, but in fact doing something else altogether. She couldn't ascertain whether he was reading or studying Wittgenstein's works or works on Wittgenstein's works, or not doing something else entirely, like having an affair, eating fast food or dealing drugs, nonetheless she would bet he was indeed reading some of Wittgenstein's works or some works on Wittgenstein's works, not only because he hadn't ever shown any signs of having an affair — no trace of strange perfumes on his clothes or skin, no lipstick blotches and similar clichés —, nor of having been eating fast food — he was still lean and had no grease stains on his clothes or similar clichés —, nor of having been dealing drugs — he wasn't suddenly buying expensive goods, he had no bruises or broken ribs and similar clichés —, but also because he seemed to be reading Wittgenstein's works and possibly works on Wittgenstein's works faster than the time he spent at home would allow him to read those same Wittgenstein's works and works on Wittgenstein's works, even taking into account all the time she spent away from home banging Mercier or doing some other activity and she didn't see him reading. He was a slow reader and had to take notes on and reread several passages to understand what he had just read, this she knew, for they had been married for many years and also because he himself usually told her that that was the case, meaning he used to tell her he was a slow reader and needed to re-read several passages to understand them, mainly passages from Wittgenstein's works, perhaps not so much from works on Wittgenstein's works, though definitely from Wittgenstein's works, and he couldn't keep his mouth shut about it, he was always bragging about reading Wittgenstein's works, with a special focus on the *Tractatus*, so she assumed he was reading Wittgenstein's works each time he lied to her and said he was working late in the evening. Mercier too had remarked he'd often find him reading, yes, reading with his shoulders covered with dandruff. She just couldn't understand why her husband lied to her, since he could simply tell her he wanted to read, whether or not at home, as she had never ever been opposed to his readings, in fact she was pleased with them, only annoyed at his snobbish petulant remarks in the morning, at lunch, at dinner, when she got into bed she'd find him reading with a pair of glasses, Anderson had bought a pair of eyeglasses although he had no visual problems, Anderson had bought a pair of eyeglasses especially conceived for old people whose eyes got sore from reading when, truth be told, his eyes didn't get sore at all, he had perfect vision, could shoot a criminal from a mile away, but that's a mere hypothesis, as he had never shot at a criminal, neither from a long nor from a short distance, though he might possibly shoot a criminal from a mile away, especially if Anderson were standing on a place high above the eventual criminal, and if the eventual criminal were standing, sitting or lying still, not moving, then it would be easier, nevertheless he might be able to shoot the eventual criminal even if they were both moving too, the most important factor being the visual contact with the target, anyway, hence the need for visual acuity. Madame Anderson got pissed-off every time she saw her husband, albeit she felt somewhat relieved whenever she saw him wearing those ridiculous glasses, as she felt less guilty for having an affair with Mercier. She would get back home smelling a bit of Mercier and upon finding her husband reading Wittgenstein's works or works on Wittgenstein's works she would sigh and glance at him with a derisive smile not short of a profound contempt but also of self-satisfaction for avoiding all sense of guilt, for she couldn't feel guilty of betraying Anderson when she saw him reading Wittgenstein's works or works on Wittgenstein's works wearing those glasses, not due to those same Wittgenstein's works or works on Wittgenstein's works, but because she couldn't stand those pretentious useless ungraduated glasses of his, not that she had anything against his readings, so much so she couldn't understand all his secrecy and hiding, even though she could use his lies to her advantage, thus meeting up with Mercier. Despite these benefits, she couldn't but wonder why he did hide from her his need of some time alone reading, though she suspected he feared finding her at home and available to love. He clearly couldn't care less about making love to her. Anderson wasn't indeed interested in establishing intimate contact with his wife. He was obsessed with Wittgenstein's work, and he was interested solely in his work or philosophical system, not in his life or in any kind of biographical details. He knew Wittgenstein had been an Austrian philosopher, but he had never known Wittgenstein had built a house for his sister, whether with his own bare hands or not, though improbably with his own bare hands. Detective Anderson found out about that curious or irrelevant detail of Wittgenstein's biography at the lecture, first during the lecture and later in the men's toilet of the auditorium, where he met the so-called second attendee, who was mocking the so-called first attendee. Nevertheless, this odd detail didn't exactly, as far as he knew, affect his way of reasoning, contrary to Wittgenstein's philosophical system as per summarized in the *Tractatus*'s first propositions. He had learned these propositions by heart, reciting them to himself like a mantra, until he had incorporated all their hidden and obvious teachings and lessons into his own mind and behavioural matrix. Henceforth, the world had become simpler for Anderson. He was happier.

As regarding Didier H. and his relation to the blonde 29-year-old woman, Anderson had already concluded the following:

The premise that Didier H. might have killed the woman is an atomic fact, thus logical or, in short, a logical entity. Therefore, its possibility must already lie in it. And as a logical entity is not merely possible but also a fact, then the premise that Didier H. might have killed the woman is a fact. Being the facts in logical space the world itself, it follows suit that if Didier H. might have killed the woman, then he in fact had killed the woman. According to a simpler formulation:

Didier H. was alive when the 29-year-old woman was still alive.

Didier H., alive, could have killed an alive 29-year-old woman.

Didier H. might have killed the 29-year-old woman because he had the possibility to kill her.

Thus he had killed her.

Why?

Because he had the possibility to kill her.

Why did he have the possibility to kill her?

The fact that he *had killed* her proved he *could have* killed her, of course.

And the fact he *had killed her* proved he might indeed have killed, which contained the *possibility of killing her*.

As nothing is accidental in logic, a logical entity cannot be *merely possible*, hence, all *possibilities are logical facts*.

Therefore, as the premise *Didier H. has killed the 29-year-old woman* is a logical entity, then it is also a *logical fact*.

Anderson concluded that Didier H. had, *logically*, killed the woman.

Why? Because he might have killed her.

Why might he have killed her? Because he did kill her.

Anderson smiled at Didier H.'s latest question. "How so?" He wouldn't explain all his systematic thinking to Didier H., he had neither the time nor the patience required to teach him logic.

"You could have killed her, right?", he asked, instead.

"What do you mean?"

"You were alive two days ago, right?"

"Hmm… yes, I was", Didier H. said.

"You were alive before your neighbour died, right?"

"Yes, I sure was."

"So, you acknowledge that you two were both alive before she died."

Didier H. seemed a bit confused. Anderson smiled at him and pointed to the tape recorder.

"Yes, we both were alive before she died."

Silence. Anderson grabbed his pen and took down some notes. Mercier wasn't following his partner's reasoning, which wasn't surprising, considering how Mercier used his free time, having a romantic affair with Madame Anderson among his occupations, but not only that, yes, he focused on too many activities instead of reading and studying Wittgenstein's works or at least works on Wittgenstein's works, hence not deriving the same teachings and building the same *corps d'intellect* as his partner Anderson, who scribbled some notes so he wouldn't lose track of his own dialectical train of thought and perfect syllogisms. He even drew some diagrams and geometrical figures to logically-embellish the paper sheets.

Didier H. was alive when the victim was alive.

The victim was alive when Didier H. was alive.

An alive person can kill another alive person.

The victim was dead.

The victim had been killed by someone.

The victim had been killed by someone *alive*.

Didier H. was alive before and after the victim's death, and therefore when she was dying.

As he was alive before and after the victim's death, and when she was dying, Didier H. could have killed the victim.

The premise *Didier H. could have killed the victim* is a logical entity, thus a logical fact.

Hence, Didier H. had killed the victim.

Didier H. was a murderer because he was alive.

Didier H. was a murderer because he could be a murderer.

Anderson was pleased. Mercier sighed, he drummed his fingers on the table, Didier H. looked at the tape recorder and waited.

"You were alive when your neighbour the victim was alive", Anderson insisted.

"Yes, I already said I was, of course."

"So you killed her."

"What?", Didier H. was flabbergasted.

"You killed your neighbour."

"No, I didn't."

"But you were alive."

"Yes, of course I was alive!"

"Then you killed her."

"What? No, no, I didn't."

"But you just confessed you were alive when she too was alive."

"I didn't confess that."

"You didn't? Are you saying you weren't alive before she died?"

"No, I am not. I was alive, of course."

"And you were alive when she died."

"Sure I was."

"So you murdered her."

"Who? Me? What? I didn't kill anyone!"

"We're not talking about anyone or some-one, we're talking about your neighbour from the third floor, a blonde 29-year-old woman, Mademoiselle Forrestier."

"Yes."

"Yes, what? You did kill her?", Anderson asked. Mercier sat on the edge of his chair and leaned over the table. He still couldn't understand what Anderson intended to do, but he was all ears now.

"No, I didn't kill her!", Didier H. cried.

"So you weren't alive two days ago?", Anderson proposed.

"Of course I was alive, how couldn't I be?"

"Then you killed her."

Didier H. remained silent, pondering how he should reply.

"I didn't. I don't understand why you keep insisting", he said at last.

"Don't you believe a person can only be murdered by another person? Isn't that what it means to be murdered? To be killed by *another* person?"

"Yes, of course."

"One can't be murdered by a dead person, nor by an inanimate object, nor even by an animal. That wouldn't be a murder. One must be killed by another person. And that person must be alive. Right?"

"Yes."

"You were alive when your neighbour died."

"I was indeed."

"What were you doing two days ago?"

"I was working. I worked till late in the evening."

"Yes, you were alive."

"I was."

"Some witnesses can confirm they saw you, certainly, and that you were alive."

"Certainly."

"Can you name those witnesses?"

Didier H. pondered for a moment.

"I can. But I need to check my notebooks."

"Do you? Why?"

"I can't remember most clients' names."

"Why is that?"

"I have many clients. I can't remember them all."

"But you just said you can't remember *most* clients' names."

"Yes…"

"You didn't say you can't remember *any* clients' names."

"Yes, but… what does that have to do with the case?"

"Everything. Everything has something to do with the case. Am I not right, Mercier?", Anderson asked, and he poked his partner with a finger.

"Yes, yes, you're right", Mercier answered, you're right your dumbass I hope you wrap this up soon I'm getting hungry, Mercier thought to himself while he scratched his legs, he stopped scratching his legs, first one, then the other, he sighed, Anderson smiled, he resumed the inquiry.

"So, you do remember the names of *some clients*", he said.

"I guess so, yes."

"Why do you remember some names and not others?", Anderson insisted.

"I don't know."

"How can you not know? Why do you recall some names and not others?"

"Some clients have stranger names. I also have some frequent clients whose names I end up memorizing, of course."

"And the witnesses who might confirm you were alive don't have strange names. And they aren't frequent clients, either. Isn't that quite odd?"

"Odd? No. Most people don't have strange names. And most clients are not frequent."

"They aren't? Right. But what's a frequent client, can you tell me?"

Didier H. asked if he could drink some water.

"Can I have some water, please?"

Mercier got up from his chair and went out of the room to fetch a glass of water.

Anderson insisted: "What's a frequent client, then?"

"Hmm. A client who calls a few times."

"A few times: how many?"

"I don't know. A few times, several times."

"You don't know. Odd."

"That's not odd, I just don't know. There's no specific number of calls to determine if a client is frequent, is there?", replied, furious, Didier H.

Anderson drummed his pen on the table.

"And what kind of services do you deliver to those frequent clients?"

"Well, all kinds of services. Whatever's needed."

"Do you fix broken pipes?"

"If needed, yes, of course."

"Can a client be a frequent client if they call you to only fix their broken pipes?"

"Yes, sure", Didier H. "But who would call me to fix only broken pipes?", he added, but he immediately regretted what he had just said.

"Oh, you'd find it odd, would you?"

"No. Yes, maybe. It's never happened; I think."

"Never ever? It's never happened in the history of plumbing?"

"I don't know…"

At this moment, Mercier arrived with a glass of water in his hand, which he put on the table. Didier H. drank it.

"Thanks", he said.

Mercier sat down again in his chair. Didier H. breathed deeply.

"Do you have an encyclopaedia on the History of Plumbing, perhaps?", Anderson insisted. "Does such a thing even exist? The Annals of Plumbing? The Ins and Outs of Plumbing Craft since the Middle Ages?"

"I don't know…", Didier H. replied, Mercier staring at him, then at Anderson, he couldn't make head or tails of that Plumbing History, the Annals of Plumbing, whatever it was, Mercier wasn't the greatest lover of literature or books in general, one already knows that, contrary to his colleague, he had never read Wittgenstein's works or works on Wittgenstein's works, though one can actually only assume that and not indeed ascertain that, as one knows solely, *in fact*, that he did not read Wittgenstein's works or works on Wittgenstein's works while Anderson was reading Wittgenstein's works or works on Wittgenstein's works, and this only on certain occasions, as when he was kissing and making love to Anderson's wife, thus only not whenever Anderson was reading Wittgenstein's works or works on Wittgenstein's works and he, Mercier, was banging Anderson's wife, and one can't infer he wasn't reading Wittgenstein's works or works on Wittgenstein's works at all while Anderson was indeed reading them but he, Mercier, wasn't banging Anderson's wife, be it each time she went out to engage in other activities, be it each time Anderson was reading at home while his wife was home. Nevertheless, making use of Anderson's take on logics, the possibility of Mercier having never read Wittgenstein's works or works on Wittgenstein's works turns into a logical entity and henceforth *a fact in the world*, thus Mercier had never read Wittgenstein's works or works on Wittgenstein's works.

Anderson renewed his attacks: "You don't know? What don't you know? Or rather what do you know? You can't even tell me the names of witnesses who can state that you were alive two days ago."

"I can check my papers and give you the names", Didier H. replied.

"Whose names?"

"Well, those of my clients from two days ago."

"What do I want them for?"

"What? Are you… Sorry, I don't understand."

"What is it you don't understand?"

"Why you don't want the names of my clients…"

"They're quite irrelevant to this case, aren't they?"

"Who? My clients? But…"

"Not your clients. You clients' names."

"But…", and Didier H. could say no more.

"Now, you were alive two days ago, as that is obvious", Anderson declared.

"That's what I've been telling you!"

"So you killed your neighbour."

"No, I didn't."

"But weren't you alive?"

"Yes, I was."

"So you must have killed her."

"I… fail to grasp your reasoning."

"You were alive. Your neighbour was alive. We have ascertained she must have been killed by an alive person. You yourself admitted that. And as you were alive when your neighbour was still alive, then you could have killed her, right?"

"Well, I could have, but I didn't."

"Of course you did. If it was possible for you to kill her, then you must have killed her. The possibility of you killing her is a fact. Otherwise it wouldn't be logic."

Didier H. opened his mouth to speak. He couldn't say a word. He lacked the necessary skills to rebuff Anderson's attacks. Moreover, he recurrently thought about the pipe dripping water in his client's house… a frequent client… who often called him due to rotting chewed up pipes full of holes… always the beavers' fault… he requested Didier H.'s services every time he got a hole in a pipe… though not only to fix pipes with holes… once that client had dropped his dentures in the lavatory… he had other draining problems… several issues with his faucets… the cleaning lady seemed to break them easily… she was a true colossus, she pulled faucets out of the sinks and bathtubs… with a single touch… he was a good client, despite ignoring all of Didier H.'s recommendations regarding the piping conditions in his house… he shouldn't live so near the river… or try to keep beavers in his home… in the back plot… which was more of a forested field than a garden… but all these considerations were pathetic, they were nothing compared to the true pathos of life, the sadness of human existence, for Didier H. thought over and over again about the university student who *allegedly* wanted nothing to do with him, she had indeed told him more than once she didn't want to have anything with him, and Didier H. would comply with her wishes, he wouldn't stalk or harass her, though some years later he would eventually kill a woman *quite similar to the university student* he had had an infatuation with, as written by a journalist and picked up by the public promotor during the trial, which went quite under the radar because by then, when Didier H. was on trial for murder, other issues concerned the public and the media, but in the 1990's Didier H. had yet to become a murderer, he was an innocent man, he tried to defend himself, he took a deep breath and mustered up all his eloquence.

"But being alive is not sufficient to say that I killed her. I had to be alive to kill her, but I didn't have to kill to be alive", he replied.

Anderson was taken aback for a moment. Mercier smiled, he sensed the tension getting hold of his partner, Anderson wasn't ready for a truculent reply. He himself was facing some doubts as to whether he could point to Didier H. as the murderer, as the notes he took down on a piece of paper may confirm.

Didier H. didn't kill the woman.

Didier H. is innocent.

Didier H. didn't kill the woman because he's innocent.

Didier H. is innocent because he didn't kill the woman.

Anderson found this dialectical construction solid enough to counterbalance his other way of reasoning. However, Major Rawls wanted results, all the department wanted to see some results, Canadian citizens wanted to see some results, the government wanted to see some results, and this new conclusion, as logical as it may be, wasn't in the least as useful to this purpose as the previous one, on which Anderson had based his entire inquiry up till now. He proceeded to interrogate Didier H.

"Well, you didn't have to kill anyone to be alive, but you were alive, weren't you?"

"I was."

"That much we can rely on. Nonetheless you can't give us any names of witnesses who might testify to you being alive."

"I can't. Not right now, anyway. But I can do it later."

"Later. And you killed her."

"I didn't. I won't say I killed her, because I didn't. I know you want me to say I did kill her, but I didn't."

"You did."

"I didn't. And I think it's time to go, or maybe I should call a lawyer."

"You can call a lawyer. But first let me ask you something."

"What?"

"Let's say you didn't kill the woman."

"I didn't, that's what I've been telling you."

"Let's just imagine you didn't, alright. But why didn't you speak to her the first time you saw her?"

"I already told you I didn't know her, she was a stranger."

"Then she wasn't a stranger the second time you saw and talked to her? Or was the second time you saw her actually the second time you saw her? Perhaps you had seen her on more occasions, and the second time you saw her wasn't the second time you saw her, but the third or fourth or fifth."

"It was the second time I saw her. I have no reason to lie."

"You don't? But you must admit it's odd the way you presented yourself."

"I don't think it is. I don't agree with you."

"Even my partner here, Mercier, agreed you acted strangely. At least according to your statements."

"I acted normally, like most people, I guess."

"By telling her only your surname?"

"Yes."

"Why did you only tell her your surname and not your first name?"

"My God, I already told you why."

"You didn't. You only told us you had only mentioned your surname."

"Most people act like I did."

"According to who?"

"I don't know. Common sense? It's the usual way people present themselves."

"Why do you think it's the usual way of presenting oneself?"

"Is that relevant to this case?"

"She was murdered."

"I didn't murder her."

"We're still investigating it. Why didn't you tell her your first name, also?"

"I didn't tell her."

"Yes, I know you didn't. I asked you *why* you didn't."

"It happened that way."

"Did it? Because you have said that's the normal way of someone introducing themselves to someone else. And now you say it happened, just like that."

"And so what?"

"If it's something normal, it shouldn't happen just because. Like it was due to mere chance."

"Some things do happen just because."

"Like what? Which things?"

"Like holding a door open for someone. I don't know."

"Did you hold a door open for someone?"

"Yes. Well, we all do at some time, right?"

"Who did you hold a door open for?"

"I… I don't know. Neighbours? That's not the point…"

"Neighbours you knew for a long time? Or still strangers?"

"Neighbours. My neighbours."

"Dcfinc neighbours."

"People who live nearby. My neighbours are the people who live in my building, for example."

"Did you hold a door open for people who lived in your building?"

"Sometimes, yes."

"How often?"

"I don't know. Whenever it happened. It's not exactly a regular occurrence."

"So, according to you all of the people who live in you building are your neighbours. How do you know they live in your building?"

"How do I know? Sorry, I don't understand your question."

"Does the postman or postwoman go in and out of your building?"

"Our mailboxes can be accessed from the street."

"Ok, but does he or she go in and out of the building? To deliver a package or, let's say, get a signature."

"Yes, sometimes, I guess. I'm mostly out during the day."

"Is it a postman or a postwoman?"

"Who?"

"The employee from the postal services who goes in and out of your building."

"It's a postman."

"Then you have seen him."

"I never said I hadn't."

"You said a few moments ago you're mostly out during the day."

"Yes, mostly. But not always."

"When are you home during the day? On which occasions?"

"At weekend."

"There's no postal delivery at the weekend, as far as I know."

"Yes, sure there isn't. Unless it's an express special delivery, I think."

"Do you often receive express special deliveries at the weekend?"

"No, I don't."

"So, how regularly do you receive express special deliveries at the weekend?"

"I don't receive them at all."

"Then how do you know one can receive express special deliveries at the weekend?"

"I don't really know. I assumed one could get them. Nothing more."

"You assumed it."

"Yes."

"And you're never home on working days."

"Rarely. I work from Monday to Friday, occasionally on Saturday morning. Sometimes I get a day free, but seldom."

"I'm asking you once again: then how do you know it's a postman and not a postwoman who delivers the mail to your building?"

"I've seen him."

"But aren't you working when he shows up?"

"I am, but I've seen him on my days off. And when I'm on holidays."

"Do you spend your holidays home?"

"In part, yes."

"And don't you live on the second floor?"

"I do."

"And doesn't the postman leave the mail on the ground floor? In the mailboxes, right?"

"Yes, he does. Unless he needs to deliver a big parcel or to get a signature from someone."

"What kind of signature?"

"Oh, you know, when one gets signed-for registered mail."

"So you do receive big parcels and signed-for registered mail when you're enjoying your days off?"

"No."

"If not, how can you see and *recognize* the postman? Do you spend your days off and part of your holidays idling on the ground floor?"

"No. I go down whenever I need to leave. But I meet him sometimes."

"Isn't that a funny coincidence? That you, by mere chance, get to meet the postman when you leave home, despite seldom being home on working days?”

“I don’t know if it is.”

“You don’t know if it is a coincidence. So you do meet him intentionally.”

“No, I don’t meet him intentionally… And… I fail to grasp how…”

“Then you meet him by mere chance?”

“Yes, of course.”

“And, anyways, seldom meeting or perhaps merely glancing at him on rare occasions, you somehow have managed to get a clear picture of the postman, recognizing him among other strangers as indeed the postman who usually if not always distributes letters and packages and all kinds of mail in your building and possibly in the surrounding area?”

“Hmm, yes, I…”

“Either you are a skilled observer with a keen memory, or you do see him more often than that.”

“I don’t know that I’m a skilled observer… Maybe I see him more often on my holidays. I don’t understand what this has to do with…”

“How do you recognize the postman?”

"How? Well, it's him. He wears a postal vest, after all…"

"So, if one of your neighbours, let's say Madame Aubert, do you know her?"

"Yes, I do."

"Well, let's say she suddenly began wearing a postwoman vest, would you start seeing her as a postwoman?"

"No, that's not…"

"You'd have thought the murder victim was a postwoman had she wore a postal vest?"

"No. I mean, I might have thought so, on the first occasion I met her."

"Not if you met her for a second time?"

"Well, if she was wearing a postal vest, yes, maybe I'd…"

"Would you possibly hold the building's main door open for the murderer if he or she was wearing a postal vest?"

"What? For the murderer?"

"Perhaps you held the door open for him the day he killed your neighbour. Unless you yourself killed her, of course."

"That's ridiculous."

"What?"

"What you've just said."

"I presented two hypotheses: that you held the door open for the killer, and that you might be the killer. Which one of them do you find ridiculous?"

"Both."

"Would you recognize the killer?"

"What? How would I recognize him?"

"So you might indeed have held the door open for him or her, granting him or her access to the building."

"I didn't let him or her into the building!"

"How do you know? Do you know who killed your neighbour?", Anderson asked, reaching for his paper and pen. Mercier seemed to wake up a bit, he had been dozing off for some time.

"No, I don't know who killed her", Didier H. replied, out of breath.

"Then was it you who killed her?"

"Oh god, no."

"A man with your criminal record… Are you sure?"

"Yes."

"You have been sentenced to prison for assault."

"That happened many years ago. It has nothing to do with this."

"Are you sure?"

"I am."

"Did you kill Mademoiselle Forrestier?"

"No, I didn't."

Didier H. was about to give up trying to defend himself and just confess he had killed his neighbour and move on to get back to business, driving to his client's house and fixing the pipe. Nevertheless, he thought he might be incarcerated for the whole day or even for years before someone might indeed further investigate the case and conclude he was innocent, though all proof pointed to his innocence, including his alibi, obtained whilst working in his clients' houses. However, he did in fact consider for a few seconds confessing to the murder and putting an end to that inquisitory, as he had done several years before, when he had been sentenced to a few months of prison for assault, despite not believing — then and now — he had in fact assaulted anyone. The way he saw it, he had simply reacted to an aggression, he was leaving a bar after an unsuccessful advance on a university student, he had been rejected and

had followed the mentioned student when she
had left the bar, him on her heels, she had met
her boyfriend outside, she had been waiting for
him together with a friend, her friend had left
fifteen minutes before, she went   outside,
Didier H. followed her, she waved to a man and
whispered something after the man kissed her,
she pointed Didier H. out to her boyfriend, she
said that man had been harassing her, look, that
jerk harassed me he didn't leave me in peace
what a moron, then her boyfriend said oh is that
so motherfucker, and he got up close to Didier
H. with a threatening posture, Didier H. had
stopped moving once he saw the university student kissing the man, he at once grasped that
her boyfriend wanted to punch him, hurt him a
bit, it's a male thing, men sense it immediately,
there's a female to impress let's impress her
punch one another maybe show some bonho-
mie and joie de vivre while doing it be a gentleman whenever you kick another gentleman's
genitals crunch them under your feet say a few
witty words a clever joke show them the lady
and other people around watching the spectacle
you're in charge at least if you have the upper
hand if don't pretend you accept it all with

verve don't let them see you going down, this and much more running through Didier H.'s mind but in a compressed way, *attack, punch the motherfucker*, he grabbed the other guy's neck, the other guy tried to punch him, Didier H. was prone to act quickly, he could stop a flood in a matter of seconds, he grabbed that neck with all his strength, could have broken it, he didn't break it, almost strangled the guy, the university student was crying and yelling for help, her boyfriend fell to the ground, Didier H. kicked him, broke two of his ribs, later he was accused and convicted of assault, that's what stained his criminal record and was still aggravating his situation within the sphere of law, Detective Anderson pulled out Didier H.'s criminal record, he had it ready in case he needed it, he prepared to resume talking, cleared his throat, suspended his speech for a while, he still didn't speak. Mercier was now feeling tired of this tedious interrogation, and yawned. Major Rawls had passed through the interrogation room door twice, both times he had stopped in front of it wondering if he should knock or just to move on, now he stopped at the door for a third time, truth be told he wanted to get out of here, this station's atmosphere is redolent of unpleasant miasmas, he thought, I can't stand this station and the people working in it because of theses horrific hazes coming off walls ceilings floors doors I shouldn't touch this door anyway I must knock and see how's it going, he wanted to knock on the door and see how the interrogation was going, he didn't believe in Anderson's and Mercier's skills, they were both dimwits, Anderson with his readings, Mercier womanizing, everyone at the department knew Mercier was having an affair with Anderson's wife, even Major Rawls acknowledged the existence of a love-related affair between Detective Mercier and Detective Anderson's wife, a fact in itself quite irrelevant to Rawls, he'd rather go out and play golf, as a young officer he thought playing golf would be boring, all other top and middle-management officers played golf, he had played tennis in his teen years, he didn't play golf, but then he had to play it for his career's sake, people kept hinting that he should go out and play golf at the club such-and-such, at last he took their advice and began connecting with all kinds of top brass, he had to buy them some whiskies and whatnot, the expense was worth it despite his wife complaints, we never go out anymore you keep spending money in golf clubs and all your free time with your new friends, they're not my friends!, he would say, indeed they were not, there were neither friends nor free meals in that world of his, perhaps in someone else's world there were friends, Rawls on the other hand couldn't find any, he put all his effort into being a good golf player, now he didn't exactly wish to play golf, he'd rather go home and sleep, rest in a good armchair in front of the fireplace, enjoy a few hours without his wife, she was an American… another American… an American woman… she was still exhilarated by Bill Clinton's victory in the presidential election… almost three weeks had passed since his re-election and still she couldn't shut her mouth about Clinton… she was a hardcore fan of Mr Clinton… from then on the world would get back on the right track… or proceed on the right track… she could sense a renewed good relationship between Bill Clinton and Boris Yeltsin… she had a feeling… some gut feeling deep inside her… really inside her… Rawls had feelings too… Darling, maybe they'll get along again, yes, and booze around…

she was disgusted with his remark, wouldn't allow him into their marital bed… she had even adopted two more cats, two cats adding to the already house-inhabiting three cats, making it a total of five cats… them yes, she allowed them onto their marital bed… she'd go to bed very early in the evening… before Rawls arrived home and ate dinner… five cats on the bed… often fewer than five… four cats and Madame Rawls, three cats and Madame Rawls, two cats and Madame Rawls, one cat and Madame Rawls… sometimes yes, five cats and Madame Rawls… also five cats and no Madame Rawls, four cats and no Madame Rawls, three cats and no Madame Rawls, two cats and no Madame Rawls, one cat and no Madame Rawls… seldom no cats at all… at least one cat, even with no Madame Rawls… Major Rawls would find the bedlinen covered in cat fur… he had to sleep amidst all that fur… the worst part was listening to American television broadcasts… thankfully the elections were over now… so he'd rather be playing golf… besides, he needed to play more if he wanted to reach the top and become the supreme police commander in Montreal, then he might finally buy a new house and add an extra bed to their room or, better still, buy a house with *two bedrooms*, one for his wife and one for him, not that he couldn't do that already in their current house, for it comprised three bedrooms, one living room and one dining-room, though they used only one of the bedrooms as a bedroom, the other two had been refurbished for other purposes, one was an office, the other one actually a bedroom, but a guestroom indeed, so it was used only as a bedroom for guests such as Rawls's parents-in-law, who lived in northern Québec, his father-in-law was polite, his mother-in-law a quiet lady, but his wife went completely mad whenever she had her parents visiting, Madame Rawls wanted everything to be perfect, the house had to be shining from top to bottom, and he couldn't stand her screams and yells and reprimands, so he needed a bigger house to accommodate his in-laws in decent conditions, he needed a new house to use at least two rooms as bedrooms, one for him, the second for his wife, he didn't need any more bedrooms, they didn't have kids, he only needed two bedrooms and perhaps two guestrooms, a big guestroom to accommodate his parents-in-law, perchance a second guestroom to accommodate more guests, but definitely he could manage with a new bedroom, a house with two well established bedrooms, as he didn't want to share his nights and intimacy with his wife, whom he already found a little repulsive *before* the American presidential election in which Bill Clinton had been re-elected, but whom he found even more repulsive *after* the American presidential election in which Bill Clinton had been re-elected, since he was flabbergasted with his wife's reactions to the political campaign and the Presidential election, he had never imagined his wife could be such a passionate follower of politics, he wondered if it might be only a Clinton-oriented enthusiasm, as in fact she hadn't shown any political orientation or social concerns before the last two campaigns for the presidential elections in the United States, and he was shocked when she announced, at lunch one Sunday, that she intended to travel to the United States to see Bill Clinton in a rally, he was shocked and didn't say anything, one morning he went to work at the police station, left early to play golf and she was gone by the time he arrived home, he felt, in part, relieved, to a certain extent he preferred to be alone in that house where they could have two bedrooms, but where they used only one of the bedrooms as a bedroom, besides one guestroom and one office, they could have converted the office into a bedroom, or even the guestroom so seldom inhabited into a bedroom, nevertheless his wife wouldn't hear of it, he was tired, hadn't slept properly in the last weeks, Madame Rawls tossed and turned in their marital bed, they had no intimate contact between them, he'd lie down rigid as a corpse, just stop it you asshole, he thought, she would turn around and groan and whisper… what did you say?... Rawls would lift his upper body supporting himself on an elbow… what are you whispering?... she'd keep whispering… she was fast asleep though… dreaming and sleep-talking… she must be dreaming of Bill Clinton, Rawls would think… hey, Eve… and she would toss and turn again, he sighed, gave up talking to her… next night he'd repeat the process, again to no avail… he couldn't determine for sure if she was dreaming of Bill Clinton, despite all his efforts, he had no way of ascertaining whether or not she was dreaming of the current president of the United States Bill Clinton, for he had no access to her mind, and she wouldn't answer his questions. Had he access to his wife's mind or had she replied to his inquiries, Major Rawls would perhaps have discovered if she were dreaming of the current President of the United States, but he had neither access to her mind nor to her answers — sincere or insincere as they may be —, and this had been disturbing his sleep and moreover his digestion and even his golf playing skills. He could not rest until he found out if his wife were dreaming of Bill Clinton, and with this chest-compressing anguish enveloping him he stood motionless, one hand on the doorknob, in front of the interrogation room door. IIc finally opcncd thc door without knocking.

"How's it going?", Major Rawls asked once inside the room.

Anderson gave a start, Mercier straightened in his chair, Didier H. turned his head around, glanced at the newcomer, Major Rawls closed the door behind him, paced the floor, reached the table, noticed the tape recorder on it, the tape was turning round and round inside the little black device, good, he thought to himself, these idiots turned it on at least, he proceeded to think to himself, he smiled at his detectives, two morons, he was relieved to know they had at any rate turned on the tape recorder, it had happened before that they hadn't turned it on, they had lost hours and hours of interrogation work and the tape recorder was not on, on a few occasions the tape recorder had been supposedly not working due to a malfunction, however Rawls had some doubts as to whether these malfunctions had occurred *before* or *after* the interrogations, because some of the detectives, or both present, whether Anderson and Mercier or another pair of detectives, should verify if the tape recorder was working properly *before* the interrogation, thus they could at the minimum be accused of negligence, if not of *vandalism,* for major Rawls did not believe for a second that most of the tape recorder malfunctions *did not* result from premeditate criminal acts committed to hide his detectives' apparent incompetence, inasmuch as they hadn't checked the tape recorder beforehand, they were all, in fact, a bunch of criminals, they vandalised police and therefore public property without flinching, nonetheless it seemed that on this occasion they had turned on the tape recorder, as far as he could tell they had turned it on, albeit Rawls couldn't say for sure if it was turned on at all, or if it had been turned on since the interrogation had begun, perchance they had only turned it on minutes after beginning to inquire that man who was wearing wet overalls, he was dripping wet, Major Rawls hadn't noticed it the first time he had seen him in that same interrogation room, there was now a puddle of water in front of, under and behind the man's chair, Major Rawls remained silent for a moment, Anderson and Mercier gazed at him, Didier H. looked at the table, Rawls gazed intently at the pool of water spreading across the floor, perhaps the puddle was already there prior to his departure from the interrogation room back to his office, maybe there was a puddle of water, smaller or the same size as that one — he at once excluded the possibility of it having been larger than it was now, as no relevant evaporation seemed plausible indoors in that season — the first time he entered the interrogation room, he wondered if he was getting distracted, senile, were he senile, he wouldn't get that new house, but then what for, he didn't want a two-bedroom house, he longed for loneliness, to be away from people, their demands hopes expectations lust wishes complaints lamentations pains grief happiness enthusiasm admiration despise remarks, a period devoid of all altercation due to human contact, interactions between two or more humans end up in disagreements, a human contacting talking touching looking at punching kicking another inevitably brings doom upon themselves, fights become feuds rivalry hatred vengeance, he wanted to be alone, Rawls felt his detectives' eyes upon him, he tried to ignore the pool of water. Mercier had noticed the water spreading across the floor, it was indeed already there the first time Rawls had entered the interrogation room, Mercier had even observed it in some more detail when he had come back from the coffee-room whence he had fetched a glass of water for Didier H., by then the pool was expanding, now it was neither expanding nor retracting, it was the same size as when Mercier had re-entered the room, Mercier was particularly prone to observe bodies of water whatever they may be, as he was interested in writing, one day, that one script about a sunken Venice, or not sunken but flooded, as *Venice would not collapse into the lagoon*, the city would rather *be flooded by the lagoon*, anyways all bodies of water exerted a stronger or weaker power of attraction over Mercier, and he gazed at the pool stagnant in front of under behind Didier H.'s chair once he noticed how Rawls couldn't keep his eyes away from it, until Major Rawls looked away from the pool, staring at Mercier, who looked down at his hands on the table, and Rawls walked around the table avoiding the pool of water then stopping behind both detectives, facing Didier H. Rawls saw once again all the dandruff on Anderson's shoulders, he felt disgusted and, swathed by the constrained and awkward silence in the room, reflected briefly, his eyes unfocused yet seeing, it's only dandruff old skin maybe not old skin but dried grease or some dried substance I wonder what dandruff is composed of but be it what it may it's only small white particles not so disgusting as urine or faeces urine and faeces are also products of human and animal bodies remnants of biological excretion, as he knew and would later comment on to his wife, whom he would observe sleeping and groaning next to him, for Rawls human biological excretion was a natural phenomenon with nothing shameful in itself, but which humans despised in general, if one were to disregard certain paraphilias involving urine and faeces, yes, the vast majority of mankind was repulsed by both these products of excretion, urine and faeces, not out of some arbitrary displeasure, instead due to biological reasons, for these products of excretion contained dead microbes and toxic substances dangerous to human health and life, therefore it was only natural to avoid these excretion products *altogether*, as Rawls would, later that night, tell his sleeping wife, and the same could be applied to non-excretion secretions such as vomit and blood, which were not, as it is obvious, excretion products, but which may be nefarious to humans, for vomit is acidic and contains bacteria and half-digested food, blood for its part could contaminate humans with several diseases, hence our instinctive repulsion to vomit and blood, even though vomit and blood are not excretion products, so it's only natural to avoid any contact with urine and faeces, thus spoke Major Rawls to his wife Eve, although one can accept some tolerance and even *attraction* towards some excretions such as sweat and eventually semen and vaginal fluid, Major Rawls reasoned and declared to his sleeping wife, who was groaning and whispering unintelligible words, some people seem to actually enjoy sweat and vaginal juices and semen from their partners, do you hear me, Eve?, he said to his wife, contrary to other excretions as urine and faeces, and other bodily secretions and fluids such as vomit and blood, sweat and semen and vaginal juices are not dangerous, at least if licked and thus consumed in *moderation*, yes, if moderately consumed sweat, semen and vaginal juices offer no peril or relevant toxicity, as determined per scientists, Major Rawls said to his wife Eve, albeit he did not tell her who these scientists might be, nor where he happened to read that information, ingesting sweat, vaginal juices and semen doesn't seem to have prejudicial effects on people's health, do you hear me, Eve?, he asked her. Despite all his convictions regarding bodily fluids and knowing that, in fact, as far as he knew, dandruff didn't represent any major threat to human life and health even if ingested, Major Rawls felt tremendously disgusted, as he would later confess to Mercier, upon seeing so much dandruff on Anderson's shoulders. Henceforth, he looked around and came to glance at Anderson's notes written on sheets of paper spread out on the table, which contained Anderson's philosophical and logical endeavours. This I can't accept, he is reported to have told Anderson in the presence of both Mercier and Didier H. We need results and God knows I want to play golf, but I can't accept this mess, he is said to have affirmed to Anderson in the presence of Mercier and Didier H. I might have my personal tastes and inclinations, like everyone else, he said in the presence of Didier H. and Detective Mercier, while the tape recorder was on, and addressing Detective Anderson, but I simply cannot accept this utter lack of judgement and professionalism in my station, he said to Detective Anderson. I cannot accept that a detective under my command, a so-called *one of my detectives*, shows up at work to spread this loathsome substance, and I say substance for lack of a precise term for these white particles, Major Rawls declared, while the tape recorder was still on, in the presence of Anderson, Mercier and Didier H., and moreover to spread dandruff, for dandruff it was, as Mercier latter explained to his colleagues and to Madame Anderson, not only on his shoulders, which is not becoming of a detective under my command, but also all over this station, including these sheets and pieces of paper filled with notes, concluded Major Rawls, and Mercier, Didier H. and Anderson all listened to him, and his speech was recorded on tape. Thus one might assume Major Rawls was disturbed by Anderson's dandruff, spread on

Anderson's shoulders and Anderson's notes, and not so much or not at all by Anderson's notes, which he may not even had read. He may have been disturbed by Anderson's notes; however, he was genuinely more disturbed or solely

disturbed by Anderson's dandruff spread all over Anderson's notes, Mercier later told his colleagues and his mistress, Madame Anderson.

Major Rawls grabbed Anderson's papers, walked to the corner of the room and tossed them into the waste basket. Some papers fell to the floor, Rawls noticed them but shrugged, he began rubbing his hands and grinning. This is outrageous, he is supposed to have said to Anderson, according to Mercier, who was in the interrogation room facing Didier H. By then, Anderson had already turned off the tape recorder. There's water everywhere, and this situation with the dandruff has gone too far, he declared to Anderson, as Mercier later told his colleagues and his partner's wife. I want you to solve this crap, Anderson!, Rawls appears to have told Anderson, as witnessed by Mercier and Didier H.

"What crap, sir?", Anderson asked.

"You know perfectly well what I'm talking about!", Rawls said. Afterwards he opened the door and closed it with a bang.

Anderson kept silent for a moment, Mercier fiddled his thumbs, Didier H. asked if he could go now. Anderson was flabbergasted, he looked at the papers on the floor… at the pool of water… the pool was not expanding, it seemed stagnant… unless someone treaded on it… splashing water on the chair, perhaps onto the tabletop… some waterdrops would reach the remaining papers… Anderson was at a loss… all that agitation had made him forget his final conclusion… the ultimate syllogism… at least he thought it was perchance the ultimate therefore his final syllogism, which would allow him to end the 29-year-old woman's murder investigation… he had everything he needed exactly as it should be organized… in his papers… and that too would pass, should pass, shall pass, to be transformed and turned into and become another scene, a different time of the day, a day after, two days after, a date unknown, as yet was unknown to Anderson what he should do to solve the problem and the situation and the scandalous mess his superior Major Rawls had hinted at, and talked about, and discussed. In short, life was meaningless, that he knew for sure, and what else he knew with all certainty no one knows, Anderson amongst the ignoramuses, for life was but a mere succession of moments feelings thoughts accumulated over moments feelings thoughts, this Anderson sensed more than he grasped or fully apprehended. Nonetheless, whoever entering the interrogation room looked at Anderson would at once understand that a great disappointment had fallen upon him, or perhaps that Anderson had already sensed that disappointment, though only now had he noticed how his change of heart had occurred, if a change it was, and that Anderson had no stamina left to empower him to proceed in that line of interrogation, despite all the unanswered questions and the infinite new questions which may arise from the incessant enquiring as regards to who, how, when, what? executed originwards and simultaneously following new paths of doubt-leading-to-questioning. Thus he turned on the tape recorder and asked Didier H.:

"Were you in your flat between 4 and 7 p.m. two days ago?"

"No, I wasn't", Didier H. replied.

"Were you in your building between 4 and 7 p.m. two days ago?"

"No."

"Where were you at that time?"

"I was working", Didier H. replied as recorded on tape, to which Anderson answered, on his turn, with a grunt and a sigh, whilst thinking about his dandruff issue and on shampoos or other medicines and treatments he might try, as he later confessed to Mercier and, that evening, to his wife, and only this concern made him, paradoxically, relax his duties and no further investigate Didier H.'s actions and whereabouts on the murder day, for he presently asked if Didier H. had been working anywhere near his building, which he had not, then he asked him if he could tell them where he had been, even if not in detail, and thus having told them in what quarters he had been plumbing the day before yesterday, Anderson asked him whether he had any reasons to kill his neighbour the 29-year-old blonde. Didier H. hadn't any reason whatsoever to kill her. Hence, Anderson dismissed him, turned off the tape recorder and began collecting his papers. With his mouth half shut, his tongue barely moving, he asked Didier H. to call them and please inform him or any of his colleagues about his precise whereabouts on the day before yesterday, between 4 and 7 p.m., the period of time in which the murder had likely been committed, per determined by the coroner, please do call us and let us know where you were, as well as your clients' names, Anderson told Didier H., now when the tape recorder was off, but in the presence of Mercier, who subsequently described this episode to his colleagues in the cafeteria, and also to Anderson's wife, and maybe one would get a bad impression of women and even state this is a *misogynistic* narrative, for neither Madame Anderson nor Madame Rawls have played a particularly edifying role in this investigation, the former having an affair with Mercier, the latter dreaming of Bill Clinton, though as it happens no one knows what Madame Rawls dreamt of when she sleep-talked-and-moaned, for only Major Rawls knew she was dreaming of the President of the United States, no one else, as far as anyone knows no one else thought that Madame Rawls was in fact dreaming of Bill Clinton, therefore no one could assume much from Madame Rawls's behaviour, instead one could make a few conclusions from Major Rawls's demeanour, especially on his relationship with his wife, the way he saw her, but there were no women involved with Michel L. and thus one couldn't call Michel L. a misogynist, though he himself had been accused of being a misogynist by some of his former girlfriends, or better still, by some of his former girlfriends and girlfriends-to-be, for Michel L. used to add to his list of old love relationships a few women whom he had only engaged with in his *mental world*, anyway they were not relevant to the investigation, per determined by Anderson and Mercier, who were now questioning Michel L. after both detectives had picked him up the day after they had interrogated Didier H., whose alibi seemed to hold up. Michel L. was blond and tall, not fitting the description of the brown-haired man seen leaving the victim's building given by Madame Aubert and Monsieur Pereira, afterwards confirmed by Alexei and Bruce. Nevertheless, the media was pressing the police commanders, and the police commanders pressed the police investigators. Anderson and Mercier had picked Michel L. up from his workplace, they usually picked up witnesses and suspects from their workplaces, as long as their witnesses and suspects did have jobs and thus a workplace, Mercier and Anderson both used this method they had learned, each in a different class and in different years, at the police academy, where they were taught by an instructor to pick up witnesses and suspects from their workplaces, and this piece of advice they had kept with them and applied in real life, first when they still wore uniforms and did patrols, later when they both met and began working as detectives, even while they were gaining experience as junior detectives under the supervision of senior detectives they used this method, which the senior detectives, as well as the instructor from the academy, encouraged in order to *humiliate* and *dumbfound* both witnesses and suspects, mainly the latter but also the former, because witnesses could lie, too, even more than some suspects, whether they were innocent or not, some suspects who are in fact criminals do in fact *lie less* than certain witnesses, a few people may indeed testify that something is true that is in fact untrue with the intent of somehow hurting their object of hatred disdain jealousy, manifold are the reasons that impel witnesses to take action and lie. However, even honest witnesses are unreliable and can be either useful or not, for their sincerity does not equal usefulness from the police's point of view. For example, were a witness to tell the police they saw a yellow dog crossing the street just after the crime was committed, they may not been telling a lie in the sense of telling that something which did not take place did indeed take place, so a yellow dog may in truth have crossed the street, though one might not know if the dog they described to the police was indeed the same dog that crossed the street, and if they did in fact see the real dog that had crossed the street, they might want to speak sincerely and yet inadvertently lie to the police, as they may perhaps wish to tell the police about *the yellow dog* they saw crossing the street, but instead tell them about *a yellow dog* — not the same yellow dog, instead another one, which they may end up being the right dog, as the right dog should be the one that in fact has crossed the street, not only from the witness's point of view, but from all points of view or, better still, the dog that has crossed the street in an objective reality as per an unbiased factual reality independent of all points of view, that sadly appears to be inaccessible by human minds and moreover by all animal minds, as it is probable that all other animal minds suffer from the same constrictions as the human mind, and within each species there may also, probably, exist different ways of accessing reality, and even among family members, within each family, and even within the same *individual mind*, and the witness can experience and perceive the yellow dog in such a way when they are crossing the street and later, after the dog has crossed the street, experience the dog in an unsimilar way, and the same can be applied to the street *itself* and the action implied by the *dog crossing the street*. One can therefore say that witnesses do sometimes if not often recreate what they have seen or heard, or seen and heard, or neither seen nor heard, not out of pure evil, but due to the constrictions of the human mind and, in this sense, they are not to blame for any or most of their inaccuracies. As for the suspects, it was obvious they may lie, and would possibly do so, not only out of a desperate attempt to conceal their criminal activities — whether regarding the crime under investigation or any other crime they had committed and of which the police may or may not be aware of —, but also due to their *instinctive uneasiness when in the presence of authorities*, as put by the police academy instructor, or because they get shit-scared when they see a cop, as a senior detective told the junior detectives Anderson and Mercier, both training under his supervision, and when they get so scared, they begin to fear everything they say might be misinterpreted and used against them, the senior detective told them, and then start to lie, he added, for the suspects, whether or not culprits of a crime, draw back to their primeval instincts of self-defence, the academy instructor had affirmed, acting with words as they may have acted with stones back in mankind's childhood, and they do resort to every conceivable scheme and mental pattern to make the authorities and their agents sympathize with them, the academy instructor had said, including telling these authorities and authorities' agents their life stories or confide their problems and longings to them, the instructor had added, a sign of an atavism alive and well deep in man's soul, that of the fear of society, as human society and group living are the most abject and dangerous ways of living, the academy instructor had confessed, both to Mercier's and Anderson's classes, during his annual and always-repeated lecture on how to pick up witnesses and suspects from their respective workplaces, and any person mentally-skilled would avoid any contact with human society as much as possible, the instructor had added, something he himself would do too, if he had no family to support, and so police officers should take advantage of this instinctive reaction to authority and interrogate witnesses and mostly suspects when they were not expecting it, in order to catch them in all kinds of incongruencies and blunders, the instructor had affirmed, and then to press the motherfuckers till they piss their pants and make them spill the beans and then it's over, job done, as the senior detective who had supervised Mercier and Anderson had concluded.

And Michel L. was facing Mercier and Anderson, the latter more silent than usual, now disappointed with Wittgenstein's oeuvre, which had failed him, Wittgenstein's work has failed me, he had told his wife, and then grabbed a Descartes's book, which couldn't help him in the least, as Descartes and henceforth the Cartesians are two of most despicable aberrations in all of Philosophy, according to Bruce the plush donkey, Bruce had read most Western philosophers thoroughly, or most philosophers, as he would put it, as Bruce the stuffed donkey refused to accept so-called Cartesianism as a valid way of perceiving reality and obtaining knowledge. I cannot accept Cartesianism as a true valid way of reaching knowledge and wisdom, Bruce reflected and sometimes told Alexei, even though Alexei could not fully grasp what he meant, Alexei was an intelligent, even brilliant child, but he couldn't comprehend Cartesianism, which in fact Bruce could perfectly understand and even endorse and support, I understand your position, dear Alexei, as no one can fully grasp such an absurdity as Cartesianism, he would tell Alexei, not even Descartes himself could grasp Cartesianism, for Cartesianism is pure rubbish, he would say, and anyone who tells you they understand Cartesianism is lying, he'd add, and worse than understanding Cartesianism is to actually believe it and follow it as a valid way of reasoning and facing the world and the mind, if someone tells you they're a Cartesian, please do *run away from that person* as fast as possible, this I advise you to do, dear Alexei, he'd tell Alexei, and Alexei would nod, for Cartesians are not only to blame for being prey to a despicable illogical unverifiable dogmatic pseudo-philosophic system, but also for echoing such a dangerous and nature-unwise way of thinking, Bruce would add, in my opinion they should also be criminally sued for mental acts of terrorism against this planet, I mean Earth, and then Bruce would say no more about this issue, neither blinking nor nodding, for that he could not do, whereas Alexei would not pursue the conversation either, knowing far too well that he couldn't get a word more out of Bruce, who loathed Cartesians and Cartesianism. So this was the new way of thinking on which, beginning the evening before upon arriving home from that failed interrogation of Didier H., Anderson was now focusing all his brain capacity, meagre as it was, for he was reading Descartes's works and works on Descartes's works. He still had to find the means to show how enlightened he was as a consequence of these latest and yet shallow readings, but he was eager to apply them to reality in trivial though pragmatic gestures. However, the opportunity to do so seemed to escape him and, demoralized and still with dandruff on his shoulders, Anderson kept a low-profile and let Mercier do the talking, his partner often thought of writing that script on a flooded Venice but he nonetheless was no amateur philosopher, nor a great reader indeed, which would make Bruce and all of us who try to notice these little human failings assume that Mercier would probably not write a good script, as most good readers do not have a good story in them, and by no means a script, and even fewer are the non-readers with any let alone good stories or scripts in them, they can write only fripperies, the upmost shameful insignificances, and this together with Mercier's lack of curiosity and experience would upset

Bruce or any wise person who happened to know that Mercier was about to or intended to write or had already written a script, for this would certainly be another evil act of terrorism on art. Bruce had in fact acknowledged to Alexei, on several occasions, how he couldn't tolerate authors who did not read, he despised those pseudo-authors who read only what they themselves wrote and, at most, what a few of their friends wrote, and he, Bruce, couldn't tell, neither to Alexei nor to me, what he abhorred more, whether it was fact 1: those pseudo-authors had no love for literature, be it novels, plays or scripts, as he saw it, for they didn't find any solace or pleasure in reading, and therefore were incapable of writing for the sake of writing and improving art, thus possibly and probably only writing to show off and make a living out of it, or whether it was fact 2: those pseudo-authors who promoted their works, be it novels, plays or scripts, which couldn't be masterworks or even average works, but mediocre works, for lack of intellectual experience, expecting them to sell and be read or watched by the public, whereas at the same time they themselves wouldn't buy or read or watch anyone else's books or plays or films, except for a few of their friends'; so, Bruce, as he had told Alexei, found fact 1 disgusting and fact 2 equally disgusting, he confessed to Alexei, who might not have understood his disgust. Mercier, who according to Bruce, would make an awful scriptwriter, inquired of Michel L. regarding his whereabouts on the day of the murder, might it be that Michel L. was in the building at the time of the murder? Michel L. lived in the same building as the 29-year-old murdered woman, and they picked him up from his workplace. Besides studying at McGill University, Michel L. worked part-time at a café. He lived in that building in Montreal, but his flat was not his property, rather his parents', who now lived in France, and though the flat was theirs, he lived in it and was responsible for its maintenance. Michel L. had told Mercier he was at McGill between 4 and 7 p.m., he had attended a lecture and went to study at the library together with some friends, and he didn't know his murdered neighbour, he had seen her every once in a while, of course, but rarely, he didn't even know her name, he had met her a few times, not enough to *know* her, he had only moved from his parent's house, where he too had lived before they had left Canada one year ago, and with the time he spent out studying working meeting his friends going to the theatre he hadn't in fact had the pleasure of getting acquainted with the blonde, as he called her, his blonde neighbour from the third floor.

"How do you know she lived on the third floor?", Mercier asked.

"I live on the fourth floor and I always saw her coming in or out of the lift on the third floor", Michel L. replied.

Now, Anderson felt an urge to question Michel L., their new suspect, officially not a suspect, he was by no means a real suspect in the sense that they had something on him, a hint, a description, he was cooperating, seemed to have an alibi, he was blond and tall, not medium-height and brown-haired, had no criminal record, yet Mercier and Anderson needed a new suspect, both to show some work when the investigation was stale, seemingly stopped at a dead end, and to erase the dandruff affair from Rawls's mind, Anderson had admitted to his wife, because in a sense, or from his perspective, cleaning his image was more important than solving the murder as soon as possible, for there were several murders every year, surely not as many as south of the border, Canadians were a quieter and less murderous people than the Americans, he had told his wife, and they could, in truth, take their time solving this murder, though it was more conspicuous in Montreal than in the United States, but they could relax, that was his honest opinion, in his experience the police would catch the murderer if the murderer was to be found, sooner or later, whether they focused all their attention and means on solving the murder or not, whereas the murderer would escape justice if that was to be the case. In Anderson's opinion, their initial efforts were irrelevant, or at least not so important as one may believe, for many of these efforts could be exerted afterwards to the same effect, though Anderson could not prove any of this, it being only a personal theory with no rational or empirical grounds, he had confessed to his wife, perhaps that was the reason why he was feeling so attracted to Descartes and Cartesianism, but this he didn't say to his wife, though Bruce assumed as much later, as Bruce, a Cartesian-hater, couldn't help but to notice that Anderson

was perchance being seduced by Cartesianism
due to his innate instinct or propensity to contemplate rational solutions drawn out of thin air,
even though Bruce himself couldn't exactly tell
if this was the case or whether it was the other
way around, i.e., whether Detective Anderson
wasn't showing signs of an increasing discon-
nection from reality because he was reading
Descartes's works or works on Descartes's
works, notwithstanding his relation with Descartes's works was much too recent, anyway
that's what Bruce later reasoned, after meeting
and talking to Detective Anderson, and thus not
even considering Michel L.'s description of Anderson's behaviour in that interrogation room,
which Michel L. could have provided to Bruce,
despite the possibility of it not being a produc-
tive description, since Anderson remained silent for most of Michel L.'s interrogation, he
asked him only a few questions, anyway, were
Anderson to speak, Michel L. would, for sure,
productively describe him to Bruce and Alexei
and Andrei, for Michel L. was a neighbour and
an acquaintance of Bruce, Alexei, Andrei and
Babushka, and Anderson seemed to be eagerly
waiting to talk, but he didn't talk, as Michel L.

told Andrei in the presence of Alexei and Bruce. His neighbour's murder had disturbed Michel L., but not too much, only a little bit. He was minorly disturbed, as he put it. He had known his now dead neighbour at all, he had seen her only occasionally, he hadn't known her name, had had never asked her for her name, had never tried to find out what her name was, he had assumed she lived on the third floor, for that's where she came from or went to whenever he met her in the lift, he had seen her a few times in the building's lobby, but mostly coming in and out of the lift on the third floor, whether he was ascending homeward bound or descending outward bound, he had noticed her, she was attractive, he admitted to Mercier, the tape recorder was on, he could and would admit he had found her attractive, which isn't saying much and nothing at all regarding the murder, about the murder he couldn't say anything, as was recorded, he had been working and studying hard, at least he thought he was working and studying hard, spent too many hours out, once home he would sleep, eat, study and read, he was fond of books and literature, he asked if their conversation was being recorded for real,

he had always been curious about how they recorded all conversations, perhaps not all of them
were recorded, some they just took notes on,
Mercier nodded, Anderson nodded, the tape recorder was on, Michel L. proceeded to talk.

"If I have to be honest and honest I wish to
and will be as allowed me by the Constitution
and demanded by my conscience my clean
spirit I have to confess I know nothing about the
victim other than that she was a blonde you tell
me she was 29 years old and I believe you I must
believe you as I see no reason for you being as
you are representatives of the national authorities to lie to me every one knows the authorities
never lie never condone with schemes and de-
ceit don't smirk sirs I'm not mocking you I am
being sincere I'm fully aware this is an interrogation though not an official interrogation I
agreed to talk to you freely out of my own will I
could have called a lawyer not my lawyer or the
lawyer but a lawyer one has to be meticulous
when talking or writing no I don't study law I
have never wanted to study law some people
used to tell me I could be a great student of law
and a superb lawyer or judge maybe I could
maybe I couldn't I'm studying economics not

my passion my passion is literature my parents
always threatened to leave me without an inher-
itance if I opted to study literature maybe they
were right they were right indeed one can't
learn literature like one learns to craft pots and
pans and economics that's easy I can get a job
and then maybe write I myself write in my free
time I keep a few notebooks at the café yes
where I work at home too it's chaos a creative
entropy I usually try to pay attention to my sur-
roundings but of course that's one of a writer's
main skills or it should be pay attention open
your eyes listen carefully read a lot there's no
university course for that you have to read read
read and pay attention listen to people they only
want to talk they need a sympathetic ear I noticed my neighbour the blonde sure I did I
found her attractive that's not really interesting
for your investigation I believe some men and
women used to come and go from the building
I would meet them at odd hours as I bounced
home- and workwards at odd hours entropy my
life is entropic everything's entropic random
sorry I want to get to the point I got a bit nervous when you two detectives picked me up at
work I wasn't expecting this maybe I would

have expected to be sought by the police perhaps a call a doorbell ring at home not at work it
looked dramatic like a film scene I mean I guess
that was the intention to cloud my mind anyways I don't want to waste your time I mean I
guess your time must be precious I need to get
back to work good move that one with the workplace pick-up my boss will surely ask questions
you aroused that gentleman's curiosity our clients' curiosity they will ask what happened the
usual customers not the casual customers of
course I'm mainly at work or at the university I
go to some friends' no I don't have a girlfriend
what do you mean no no I have had some girlfriends never made any move on the blonde I
mean I told you she was attractive nothing else
I didn't even know her name before I heard it
in the news bulletins on tv once I got home that
night yes I mean the murder night or better still
the murder day night or the night of the day on
which the murder occurred how do I know she
wasn't murdered in the night come on I got
home in the evening I at once saw the patrol
cars the ambulance the police tape I had to show
my ID card to enter the building it was a mess
reporters cameras I also heard her name in the

news the day after we had the radio on in the café I even commented that I was her neighbour she was killed in my building I commented on this to my boss some customers my friends at the university no no professors no I don't have philosophy classes what for economics is way more important I read books in my free time not philosophy books though they're boring I prefer to deal with life real life and characters both real and imaginary I fantasize no I don't fantasize about death no more than any normal human being shall I define normal human being that's not easy one more senses and feels it rather than defines it it's not a clear mental concept normal is the usually accepted isn't it if most people ate shit pardon my language but if most people ate shit wouldn't it be normal to eat shit to be a normal human being by eating shit it doesn't mean it would be right no often minorities are in the right society can normalize all kinds of atrocities and unethical practices I'm just a student I work at a café what do I know no no I'm not defending murder or coprophagia only trying to make a point what point well I don't care much about certain details I want to be a writer I think I have it in me I didn't sense any literary potential in my late neighbour no I care for people of course like that kid from the opposite building he's always out with his donkey no not a real donkey a stuffed donkey I hear him speak to him I know his older brother Andrei he's a nice guy he used to get me some well never mind what oh yes some hmm guitar tabs yeah I used to play the guitar no no weed never he worked with me at the café for some time then he got dismissed I don't know why neither does he I guess he works at a pizzeria now nice guy I used to visit them often now it's rare sometimes but not so much anymore I guess everyone has their life it's the usual people come and go most of our acquaintances are transitory but the kid is alright too the donkey too I guess they have no mother their father is a skunk I met him several times no not around the block I met him in many places he tried to sell me VCRs and radios and stuff like that it seems he was an engineer in the Soviet Union Andrei told me his father was full of crap about KGB and CIA agents connections I don't know for sure yeah they live in the building opposite on the other side of the street above the grill restaurant it belongs to a

Portuguese he and his wife grill chicken there it smells in the staircase Andrei doesn't like to open windows he gets pissed-off because of the grilled chicken smell it stinks like charcoal really greasy the kid is always popping up or was now not so much but I really don't go there so often not anymore since Andrei left the café yeah he's a smart guy but he's not studying at the university he told me he had no money he wants to apply for a grant some Russian Soviet shit I mean I guess some post-Soviet crap something like that I can't say he's my friend a real friend you know Alexei the kid yes his brother seems a nice kid smart too their grandma is a Russian lady by the way Andrei was born in Ukraine did you know I find that interesting one day I might write about them who knows their grandpa was an engineer too many engineers in that family no not their father's father but their mother's father he died in the nuclear explosion in Chernobyl you know it's quite funny to know someone who was there their family I mean not the kid he wasn't born there just here Andrei was already born he was 8 at the time I guess he remembers some episodes juicy stuff people in trucks military convoys they left everything furniture house cats dogs books almost everything their grandpa worked there no I mean I guess they're Russian or whatever they were living in Pripyat yeah they both speak fluent French and English quite smart I told you their father too it seems a bit too much of a conman for my taste but smart one can just tell he's a genius of electronics and stuff really Andrei says he performs miracles with computers and stuff but he has issues I don't know alcohol maybe drugs women don't know for sure you must ask Andrei their grandma doesn't speak much English or French I mean I think she could but now she's senile or something so she forgets stuff all the time interrupts conversations to tell Andrei he must go to school yeah all messed-up and has some cancer I mean I guess that's what I concluded she's all messed-up I guess she's going to die anyway the kid doesn't seem to understand maybe he doesn't want to one day I saw him throwing snowballs at his grandma the old lady almost fell I mean I guess she wasn't all that sick like now she rambled a bit a tiny bit senile perhaps but it wasn't like now always sitting on the couch the kid Alexei right he was throwing snowballs at her she was soaked her jacket was soaked through it was last year yeah more or less one year ago and he was yelling Oh Babushka because they call her Babushka he and Andrei Oh Babushka is this like your Russian snow he yelled and asked she said something in Russian I guess I mean it must have been he replied in Russian too or whatever then waved at me I got closer he told me his Babushka that's what he calls his grandma she thought that Canadian snow was not like Russian snow she said snow there in Russia was thicker or harder I can't recall it doesn't matter for you I guess I mean for the investigation in my opinion it might have some literary juice I forgot to note it down immediately so I can't recall if the Russian snow was thicker or harder or thicker and harder anyway Alexei the kid kept throwing snowballs at her she was smiling and laughing he hit her twice in the face she rubbed her skin he had a backpack on you want more Russian snow he would say over and over again in French then he spoke in Russian the kid yes he surely was bedraggling his grandma with Russian snow her jacket was wet through and through then she told me in French they had to go home come over to our

place dear young man yes she remembered me
I went there once in a while poor old lady she
offered me tea she has a samovar yes good tea
yes good tea I have to visit them now that I
think about it maybe someone could have seen
the murderer from their place from their building they live on the second floor there's the grill
restaurant on ground floor a flat above it then
their flat and another flat above that I'm not saying they saw anything or someone like that guy
Pereira saw I guess that's what he's called if I'm
not mistaken Pereira yes maybe no one saw anything oh yes he did right good and my neighbour Madame Aubert oh don't worry I won't say
anything anymore if you say that I'm not the police yes sure no more words on it I swear yes I
keep notes I observe things stuff interesting
stuff people no not my neighbour about those
people I saw coming and going no nothing really
a postman yeah sure there's a postman who
comes to the building nothing special about him
what did you say how I know well he's the postman with a postal vest you know he delivers the
mail well anyway I write mostly notes about
people I meet at the university or in the café no
no neighbours except those in the building on

the other side of the boulevard the two brothers
the grandma you know it's not easy to find stuff
to write about I keep reading and reading and
observing everything has already been written
about it almost seems that way so what would I
want to write about what's there to say anymore
all styles trodden all stories told maybe this
wasn't what you were expecting I mean I guess
you were expecting some thrilling novelty some
detail no I haven't seen any average tall men
with dark hair well I have but no one I could
point out no no strange behaviour at least in my
building everything's quite normal there what
do I mean by normal well I already told your colleague the detective yes well those other neighbours they live on the other side of the boulevard you should perhaps ask them if they saw
anything you want their number I have it in my
notebook well sure you don't need it you're the
police by the way if one day I want to write a
crime novel some thriller not my cup of tea but
who knows a nice book full of cliff-hangers I
need to sell a little bit love of literature is a fine
thing but people demand answers and look for
answers in books and fiction and literature I
can't give them answers there are no answers to

be given life has no answers therefore there are no answers in literature there are no answers at least the answers people really seek there can't be any only answers people want to find but already know deep down they know them already unless they're believers if they have faith in something a higher power if they believe we're special the chosen ones we are not there's nothing special in mankind a flaw of nature so I can give them a few answers they can reach by themselves or invent a mystery and provide them a few solutions in which case I divert their attention from the essential deep questions still and ever unanswered yes ever there won't ever be any answer I can at least get some money from a good mystery a crime a thriller yes sorry no more lectures I don't want to give any lectures am simply talking we need to talk we all should talk about problems and such yes no yes my parents are abroad France exactly I mean I guess I can go now I mean I guess I don't know anything about the murder."

Michel L. didn't know anything about the murder.

He had an alibi for the presumed time of the homicide.

He had no reasons to kill his neighbour. Apparently.

Thus reasoned Mercier.

Michel L. was made to wait a couple of hours in the police station, so Major Rawls could see him and acknowledge him as a suspect, they told him hey Major look, there's our suspect, he nodded, the golf match had been a pleasure, it was a nice day for November.

Then they released Michel L.

Afterwards, Anderson and Mercier went out to eat something. They ate some hotdogs at a street stand. Mercier thought they smelled and tasted bad, Anderson agreed, but only to himself, as he was still pissed-off for not having conducted the last inquiry, having only asked a few shy questions to their suspect, so he kept quiet, he ate his hotdog and Mercier shrugged and ate his hotdog, too.

They felt sick when they were questioning Bruce.

"So, our Dad hung up that call at 11.15 a.m., and at 11.18 a.m. he said he wanted to take us for a walk."

Anderson was listening to him, though barely. Mercier came back into the interrogation room.

"Dad took us out, our Alexei and me, dear gentlemen, after he had closed the workshop. Is the tape still recording, Monsieur Detective Mercier? I see you are also not feeling ok, and your temperature is abnormal. This I can measure with no problem, no problem indeed. Our Dad equipped me with a thermal sensor, or a thermometer if you prefer. A long-distance infrared thermometer, I could shoot someone alive in the dead of the night. If I had a gun and could hold it. Look at my little arms, they're not fit to hold a gun, and I lack the capacity to move my limbs in a voluntary fashion."

Mercier looked at the tape recorder, then glanced at Bruce the plush donkey.

"Yes, it's recording."

Mercier looked at Anderson, sprawled on the floor, now trying to get up on his knees.

"Your partner Monsieur Detective Anderson is not feeling well either. And as he straightened his torso, I can see his temperature's not the best, somehow. Whither you two gentlemen go after this interrogation, pray do consult your doctors. I would say you have ingested contaminated food. You two apparently share food poisoning symptoms. I believe I'm not wrong in assuming you went to the toilet with the intention of relieving yourself of an abrupt episode of diarrhoea or vomit, or both, Detective Mercier?", Bruce said.

Anderson got up, leaned on the table.

"So, dear gentlemen, our Dad took us to eat some ice cream. He wanted to tell us about Babushka, the old croon, as he calls her. We already knew what the problem with her was, we were aware she was suffering from an oncological disease rotting her body and mind and soul away, dear detectives. Can I proceed?"

Mercier nodded but kept silent, he returned to the door but left it untouched.

"Nevertheless, now that I think about it, all this is quite irrelevant to the murder, dear gentlemen", Bruce added.

"What?", Mercier and Anderson asked in unison.

"That's right, it's not relevant at all. It's only important to our little family. But I can tell you who killed the blonde 29-year-old woman, gentlemen."

"Who? Who killed her?", asked Anderson, still leaning on the table.

"I should say you have a fever, Detective Anderson."

"Do I? Yes, maybe."

And Anderson looked at Bruce as if he were trying to look into him, but Bruce did not move, notwithstanding his speech having never been completely interrupted.

"To get all the chronology straight, though, I should on my and our Alexei's and Babushka's and Andrei's and Dad's, in short, on our little family's behalf, explain how things went from one episode to another, from the ice cream, which might appear to be refreshing but simultaneously too cold for a November day, to other occurrences. Nonetheless, the one which does concerns me and our Alexei the most is a future occurrence or episode, if one may call a future episode or event an episode or event, for it has not yet happened. But I think one may say it's an event or episode, since it's potentially an event or episode, so the idea of one event or episode occurring in the future, be it sooner or later, contains in it itself the factuality of that event or episode existing and occurring", Bruce said.

"Oh, god, please no", Anderson said.

"And that future occurrence or episode, as it possibly is going to happen and is in fact happening or has already happened as an atom of factualness in the world of the mind, which is to say, as far we know, the world of humans and for extension the world I too inhabit, because, dear gentlemen, what's the probability of a plush donkey talking and thinking in a human way and, at the same time, of enjoying some benefits or advantageous conditions provided by its internal circuits and systemic chips, fluids running through its components as blood through humans, and yes, capable of solving complex mathematical equations, just like these new computers, and I have indeed noticed you, here at this police station, lack these computers, and rely solely, as it seems, on old writing machines. Well, as I was wondering, what's the probability of a stuffed donkey like me existing, no one would believe it if they found such a description in a book or a film, and yet here I am, I do exist, and if I didn't, I would still exist as a potential thus actual plush donkey with these characteristics derived from the idea of this donkey."

"Oh, it hurts", Anderson groaned.

"I don't doubt it does, Monsieur Detective Anderson. In addition to the fever, you seem to have gastrointestinal inflammation, which fits perfectly to my suspicions as regards food poisoning. Maybe not the worst food poisoning, probably something you ate yesterday, taking into the account it's still early morning and the high probability of you two detectives not having had breakfast together, but still food poisoning I reckon."

Anderson sat down at the table, he was livid, Mercier grabbed a glass of water, drank it, he too sat down.

"I've got stomach cramps", Anderson stated.

"Does it hurt a lot, Detective Anderson?", Bruce asked.

"Yes, it…"

"Now wonder how it must hurt for Babushka! All that cancer spreading. It's a cancerous tumour, a malign mass of deformed cells multiplying incessantly, without control, within her body. It started in her lungs, the cancer. Then it spread."

"Oh, my", Mercier said.

"I believe it must be an inconvenient revelation the one allowing us, and by us I refer to
humans, and pray do concede me the cheeki-
ness of including me among humans, within
mankind, if only for my mentally impaired, if I
can state it, capacity and skills, for one can be
intelligent but still be mentally impaired if
tainted by human thinking, but as I was saying,
it must be an inconvenient revelation to
acknowledge and discover how our own — in
this instance, *yours only* — cells can multiply
and destroy our other cells and the whole body.
Yes, it must be a shock. But one must know
about it, lest one may be hindered by a veiled
reality and rendered incapable of reaching the
truth, or *a* truth, if I may say so."

Anderson and Mercier both moaned.

"So one must think about how Babushka is
suffering and in all that pain she went through
all her life. For she will soon die. This I know,
and the physicians, and Andrei, I don't doubt
that Andrei knows it. But Alexei doesn't. He's
too young and too innocent, yes, smart though
innocent, and not yet cynical enough to under-

stand how irredeemable life is. There's no salvation. And I could tell you about how our Alexei concocted a possible means of salvation to cure Babushka. He wants to travel to Mexico…"

"Please no", Anderson said, almost banging his head on the table.

"Well, am I bothering you, dear gentlemen? Perhaps you find my speech too unreal, too far-fetched. No one talks like this, of course. You surely feel even diminished when compared to me and my…"

"No, please no, I can't take it anymore. Just tell us…", Anderson cried.

"Yes, indeed, let's not bother you with the details. We need no details in life! Just get straight to business. Time is money. So, I can tell you who's the killer."

"Yes, you *must* tell us", Mercier urged him.

"Monsieur Pereira has told us about the war he fought in, in Portuguese Guinea. Once, he was spreading manure…"

"Oh, come on!"

"Yes, I'm sorry. I seldom talk to anyone, so I get lost in mental wanderings. Words and words! But in regard to the murderer, you know, I've seen him."

"Yes, we know!", both detectives said.

"The bacteria are most surely multiplying inside your gastric apparatus. You should go to the doctor."

"Yes, we will, after you tell us about the murderer!"

"There's another issue I should probably touch on here, before moving onwards. The problem with flies in our building. Flies coming up from the basement, male and female, no doubt there are a few females breeding down there, or at least one female, a queen, are they like bees or not, I wonder, one female is surely laying eggs, hundreds and thousands of eggs."

"What the heck…?"

"The basement doesn't even exist, the landlord said to Andrei, and I overheard him, as I was close to the phone, it doesn't exist on the blueprints, officially there is no basement, nothing below the ground floor. But then, who's responsible if something happens down there?, Andrei asked. What do you mean with something happening down there? Well, if someone dies in the basement, or if there is a fire or a flood, if a fire starts in the basement, who's responsible? There's nothing down there, nothing can happen. There's a basement, you very well know. I know nothing of it. Officially there are no basements or cellars in this building. But there is a basement, you can come and look, it even has a door, Andrei said on the phone. I've heard about it, sure. But I don't know anything, I can't comment on rumours, said the landlord, and I overheard him. And anyway, there's nothing on the blueprints, I can't discuss this matter with you, and he hung up."

"Please, what does that have to do with anything?"

"Yes, what, dear gentlemen? Nothing and everything at the same time."

Mercier drank some more water, Anderson belched.

"Now the blueprints were somewhere, our landlord might check them, if necessary. Nevertheless, it might be unnecessary or at least useless, checking blueprints would leave him nowhere."

"Stop with this nonsense right now!", Mercier cried.

"Yes, I will. I understand you and all the city of Montreal, and the country and the entire world want to know who the murderer is."

"Yes, we all want to know!"

"Who killed the 29-year-old blonde woman?"

"Yes. Who killed the woman?", asked Mercier.

"Well, it was a medium-height brown-haired man."

Born in 1985, João Reis is a Portuguese writer and literary translator of Scandinavian languages. He studied Veterinary and Philosophy and has lived in Portugal, Norway, Sweden, and the UK. He has five novels published in Portugal.

His first novel *A Noiva do Tradutor*, was his first work to be translated into English, as *The Translator's Bride* (Open Letter Books, USA, 2019). In 2020, it was published in Brazil (DBA). His novel *A Avó e a Neve Russa* was shortlisted for the Fernando Namora Literary Prize and has been translated into English under the title *Bedraggling Grandma with Russian Snow*. His third novel, *A Devastação do Silêncio*, was longlisted for Oceanos Literary Prize, and his fourth novel, titled *Quando Servi Gil Vicente*, was released in October 2019 and was also shortlisted for Fernando Namora Literary Prize.

Lightning Source UK Ltd.
Milton Keynes UK
UKHW010708240222
399179UK00001B/162